"*The Ashes of Cast*
of God's interve[n]
was so authentic I could hardly believe it was historical fiction. I would recommend this book to my friends."
Jeanne Hossler, Bth, Pastor Emeritus, Church of God

"'He knew in his heart it had to be done, or he would die.' Have you been at this point in your life, when action was needed, and doing something, anything, was dependent upon beliefs and deep faith? Author Norman Northrup takes the reader on an intimate journey into the life of very believable characters, a trip filled with life's crises, the painful experiences of despair, and the welcomed discoveries of genuine hope in God.

The Ashes of Castlemont chronicles the challenging story of Colonel Jonathan Stevens and the struggles he endured during and after one of our country's most significant wars. The good depicts the intense dynamics of the colonel's family and friends and the changing paths of the community in which Stevens lived during the American Civil War. At one point Jonathan asked, 'Was there really a God, or was it just a big hoax?'

The various pitfalls in the lives of Colonel Stevens, his wife Amelia, and their children Johnny Boy and Georgiana continue to focus the reader's attention upon life's tragedies and the fundamental questions of our ultimate purpose in existing on earth. 'Late at night, as she was sleeping, Amelia again wrestled with who was really in control of her life and happiness.' The story's setting in the South, the emotionally charged issues of slavery, and the destructive nature of civil war are vividly portrayed in this engaging account of personal testimony, humbled spirit, and rekindled commitment.

The Ashes of Castlemont keeps the reader wanting to join in this enticing journey with the main characters. Through the lives of an easily identifiable family, Northrup's story challenges each of us to examine our own moral purposes and works of faith, and it ends with God's blessings."

Mark J. Haddock, PhD

The Ashes of Castlemont

Norman Northrup

The Ashes of Castlemont

Tate Publishing & *Enterprises*

The Ashes of Castlemont
Copyright © 2008 by Norman Northrup. All rights reserved.

No part of this publication may be reproduced, stored in a retrieval system or transmitted in any way by any means, electronic, mechanical, photocopy, recording or otherwise without the prior permission of the author except as provided by USA copyright law.

Scripture quotations marked "NIV" are taken from the *Holy Bible, New International Version* ®, Copyright © 1973, 1978, 1984 by International Bible Society. Used by permission of Zondervan Publishing House. All rights reserved.

This novel is a work of fiction. Names, descriptions, entities, and incidents included in the story are products of the author's imagination. Any resemblance to actual persons, events, and entities is entirely coincidental.

The opinions expressed by the author are not necessarily those of Tate Publishing, LLC.

Published by Tate Publishing & Enterprises, LLC
127 E. Trade Center Terrace | Mustang, Oklahoma 73064 USA
1.888.361.9473 | www.tatepublishing.com

Tate Publishing is committed to excellence in the publishing industry. The company reflects the philosophy established by the founders, based on Psalm 68:11,
"The Lord gave the word and great was the company of those who published it."

Book design copyright © 2008 by Tate Publishing, LLC. All rights reserved.
Cover design by Nathan Harmony
Interior design by Stephanie Woloszyn

Published in the United States of America

ISBN: 978-1-60604-697-5
1. Fiction: Christian: Historical
2. Family & Relationships: Ethics & Morals
08.010.21

Dedication

This book is dedicated to my wife, Beryl, who has been my love and companion for fifty-four years.

Acknowledgments

Thank you, Jeanne, for reading and re-reading my manuscript from the beginning. To Josie, my African-American friend and prayer warrior, who gave me insight into the culture and language of that time. For Billy, who so graciously helped with the formatting from one program to another. I couldn't have done it alone. To Debbie, Vydell, and Lora for their help in the final editing.

There are many people who offered encouragement that kept me on track during the writing of this book. From the bottom of my heart I thank my family, my church family, and my many friends, and I must not forget my wife, who loved me and supported me in every way. And my editor, what would we do without them and those who actually make this book into print?

Thank you all. There is no way I can ever name everyone who influenced this book in some way, but know that you are all very special.

Foreword

You are going to love this story. It is as riveting as it is well researched. It is drawn from a pivotal time in American history that bears remembering. You will follow Jonathan Stevens, the main character, through the horrors of the Civil War, the agony of adjusting to life afterwards, and the triumph of rebuilding a life decimated by tragedy. This captivating story is a journey into self, filled with the raw emotion that stirs within each one of us as we process personal catastrophe and look for the hand of the divine revealed in the ruins.

The themes that the author develops in the book—heartache, perseverance, forgiveness, reconciliation, and the search for salvation—are part of the fabric of the human experience. This is not only the story of the characters written into the book; it is your story as well as mine. To be sure, each one of us has experienced some degree of suffering in life. We have all encountered obstacles and grave disappointments, and we are constantly confronted with the circumstances that put our courage to the test.

Will we recoil or rebound? Do we possess the necessary reserves and resolve to endure and thrive?

Norman Northrup is a gifted writer whose vulnerable allegory has left for us a treasure. He has granted us access into the shared experience of the human struggle and has challenged us not to wave the white flag of surrender. He has challenged us to fight, to search, to strive, to overcome! This story is sure to leave you better poised to face any personal challenge you encounter, and if you are currently enduring unspoken hardship, you will be greatly encouraged by this book.

Mathew Klaus, Pastor
Bachelor of Science in Speech Communications
Northwest Christian University
Eugene, Oregon

Introduction

The Ashes of Castlemont is not meant to be just another ordinary novel. My objective as a writer is to lead the reader on a journey through the turbulence of troubled waters dealing with life's crises, however big or small, and discover that there is hope and a life worth living in the future.

I have a master's degree in theology and family counseling, as well as thirty-five years experience as a pastor and family counselor. I have also seven years experience working in the prison system, part of which was in the mental ward. These experiences have sharpened my awareness of the many forms of dysfunction that confront and imprison the daily lives of our society.

Castlemont is the story of my life, as well as yours, as we struggle physically, emotionally, and spiritually to find the real meaning and purpose for which we were meant to live. I want you, dear reader, to walk with me through the pages of this book and confront the maze of our own personal denials, angers, fears, doubts, withdrawals, excuses, times of depression, feelings of forgotten memories and emotions, and the need for forgiving and forgiveness. Hopefully together we will surrender our pride and wounded feelings, in faith accept the healing powers of the Lord Jesus Christ, and receive God's saving grace and peace. May we experience the joy as we quietly see God intervene on our behalf.

References regarding cultural and ethnic names are in keeping to the era to which this book is referring and are not the practice of this writer.

The Spirit of the Sovereign Lord
is on me,
because the Lord has anointed me
to preach good news to the poor.
He has sent me to bind up the
brokenhearted,
to proclaim freedom for the captives,
and release from darkness for
the prisoners,
to proclaim the year of the Lord's
favor
and the day of vengeance of our God,
to comfort all who mourn,
And provide for those who grieve
in Zion—
to bestow on them a crown of beauty
instead of ashes,
the oil of gladness instead of mourning,
and a garment of praise instead of a
spirit of despair.

Isaiah 61:1–3

The Homecoming

Colonel Jonathan Stevens rode his tired horse dejectedly down the road toward Castlemont. He had not bathed or shaved in days, and his threadbare, multi-patched, faded Confederate uniform was almost beyond recognition. It was a warm, balmy day in May of 1865, the war was finally over, and he was going home. He rode in fear and trepidation. All along the way, he saw the casualties of the war—burned out plantations, forgotten fields, and haggard faces of those left behind. He was a changed man. He felt very old and worn out.

Before the war, he never had a real care in the world. He was born into a wealthy Southern plantation family of Scotch-Irish heritage and was the only surviving son. He was educated in one of the finest Southern universities and was well traveled abroad. He had married Amelia Siegfried, the most sought after, beautiful, and spirited of all the "Southern Belles."

She was known as a "Georgia Peach," and Jonathan knew he was a lucky man to have snared her away from all her other suitors. He worshiped the very ground she walked on. His son, Johnny Boy, had been his first dream fulfilled, and his daughter, Georgiana, was his pride and joy. But that was all over now. Johnny Boy had been killed in the battle of Gettysburg. Jonathan had lost his own right arm at Vicksburg. He was not sure if Amelia would be at Castlemont when he arrived or if she would still be with Georgiana in Atlanta. He could still visualize the battlefield and smell the nauseating stench of blood, dirt, and gunpowder. He remembered the mangled bodies of horses and men strewn everywhere in every form of mutilation. He could never forget the deafening roar of cannon and rifle fire mingled with the screaming cries of the wounded and dying. They haunted his every wakening hour and filled his nights with nightmares.

He could still remember his rifle falling as a minie ball shattered his right elbow. At first he thought the rifle had just slipped out of his hand and that the bullet had only hit his shirt sleeve because he felt no pain. Then he saw the blood soaking his shirtsleeve and felt the onset of the excruciating pain.

Jonathan would never forget the ordeal of his surgery, nor the doctor and his assistants with their exhausted, bloodshot eyes and blood-soaked aprons. He remembered the doctor telling him to get up on the makeshift operating table and how he had begged the doctor to not cut off his arm, but gangrene had already set in. He knew in his heart it had to be done or he would die. He felt he would most likely die anyway, but he had to take the chance.

He had been given some laudanum to dull the pain and his senses in preparation for the surgery. He also remembered the doctor's assistants holding him down and the agony of the first penetrating incision before he passed out.

His mind was seared with the unforgettable memory of the bitter months of recovery in the hospital surrounded by his mangled and dying comrades. His body was emaciated from infection, poor food, and sleepless nights. He was a ghost of the man who had ridden so proudly off to war from Castlemont some four years earlier. He had been so proud and determined, a true Southerner, who had been given to hot-blooded politics and a damnation of all Northern Yankees in general, with their so-called superior interfering ways. Slavery and "King-Cotton" reigned in the South, along with contempt for poor white trash and an exaggerated courtesy for women. Horseracing, playing a friendly game of cards, and a good brand of Irish whiskey were his private interests in life.

There had been a brisk, restless chivalry in Jonathan that had attracted Amelia to him. She had seen him to be a "warrior of valor" who attacked life with unhesitating zest. But that was all gone. He felt like he was a skeleton of the living dead, traveling the road of doom, wanting and waiting for a grave to swallow him up.

His heart ached as he passed plantation after plantation ravaged by Sherman's armies. It was like riding through a huge, desolate, long-neglected graveyard with naked chimneys standing as gravestones to mark the ending of the great life in the South.

The vast Georgian cotton fields lay uncultivated and now were filled with weeds and newly sprouted brush, as though sneering at what had been. The fencerows were unkempt and fallen in disarray. Occasionally he would see, or sense, haggard faces staring at him from some hiding place beside the road.

He traveled on with his mind torn between hope and fear of what had happened to Castlemont. *Will there be anything left? I wonder if Amelia will be there. Will she accept me now, being just "half a man" with only one arm? What has happened to my seventy-eight slaves? How will I, a fifty-year-old man with one arm, who has never done a day's labor in my life, farm a two thousand-acre plantation without slaves?*

What about my beautiful thoroughbred horses the slaves had hidden for me in the swampland when I left for the war? No army passing through would leave behind those magnificent animals. In fact, what about me? No one even knows I am alive.

He had sent word from the hospital to Amelia in Atlanta but was puzzled that there had been no reply. Trying to get mail through enemy lines had not been easy. He was glad she was safe with their daughter, Georgiana, and her husband, James. *But what about James? Has he made it through the war?* Evening approached, with its sunset of many changing colors drifting through the foliage of new spring leaves as he finally turned into the lane and beheld the ashes of Castlemont. Everything he had ever lived for was gone. There were no signs of life—no birds singing, no happy sounds of children playing. Plantations had been noisy places with the blacksmith's hammer clanging, dogs barking, roosters crowing, people laughing or shouting, and babies crying.

Silence. Dead silence, except for the chipper song of the mockingbird and the buzzing of the few honeybees.

THE ASHES OF CASTLEMONT

The magnificent mansion with its twin spiral staircases, marble-floored grand ballroom, the large library, and dining room—all complimented the other rooms, but it was gone. Even the slave quarters were all gone—burned to the ground. The graceful giant oaks seemed to be hanging their heads in naked shame. Anger and hatred engulfed Jonathan until he looked up and cursed God for allowing him to live to see this final total humiliation of the war.

Castlemont had been in the family for nearly a hundred years and was one of the great showplaces of the whole South. It had ranked alongside the Butler Island and Lovejoy plantations. All there was left now were the badly singed, giant, live oak trees draped in Spanish moss that had faithfully stood as sentinels along the long lane and around the mansion itself.

The huge manicured lawns were now a disheveled hayfield. Gone were the hedges and fences. The large flowerbeds and rose gardens were now a matted weed bed with only an occasional flower struggling to survive. It was as if some unearthly demon had swallowed it all up and spewed it out, leaving a hideous scar upon the site. There was an awesome feeling of doom about the place.

Jonathan got down from his horse and left the reins to drag on the ground. His mind again began to race. *Is anything left of the beautiful furnishings? What about the imported paintings, rugs, chairs, and settees? The lamps, pianofortes, and the dishes that graced the tables? I wonder where they might be.*

He could visualize Toby, his valet and butler, waiting

patiently to take his coat and hat and telling him where he could find Amelia and the children as always.

He wondered if any of the slaves were hiding out in the river bottoms and swamps. In the fading light, he once again surveyed the ruins of the once beautifully manicured yard and gardens. Even the beautiful red soil seemed faded as if it was also dying. Here and there a lonely flower was valiantly trying to bloom to dispel the tragedy.

A few wild ducks swam on the pond, and the evening doves sang their mournful songs to the coming of night. He trod with leaden feet as he walked about the whole area, surveying the ruins with disbelieving eyes. He could see that the white fences had been torn down, stacked, and burned. He also saw that the Yankee "Blue Bellies" had corralled their horses in the main garden plot, which had been between the big house and the barns.

Even the beautiful magnolias, roses, azaleas, and dogwoods had been chopped down or pulled up. His heart was broken. They must have known that he was a colonel to do such a thing as this. He took his anger out on the Yankees, forgetting what he had ordered done against the Yankees during the war.

There was nothing left to do but to make camp for the night under the shelter of the oaks. Since it was late spring, the nights were still cool and required the use of a fire for warmth and comfort. The only redeeming factor was that the trees were leafed out and the new spring grass made for a soft carpet over the ground.

There was not any graceful way for Jonathan to mount or dismount from his horse with only one arm. He had been right handed, and now it was so awkward with only his left arm to take the saddle off and put it on. He had mastered that problem by hooking the right-side stirrup and cinch strap over the saddle horn, and then swinging the saddle up on his right shoulder, he could boost it up onto the horse.

He finally got his horse unsaddled and picked up the halter rope to lead the animal to water. He soon discovered that even the watering trough by the barns had been destroyed. He had to admit those "damned Yankees" had been thorough in their destruction. He led the horse to the nearby pond to drink and picketed him out to graze for the night.

Jonathan gathered a few sticks and dried grass and managed, with some difficulty, to build a fire as darkness quickly settled in. The unearthly stillness of the night was broken by the cry of the nighthawks and the swooping of bats. The crickets and frogs also took up their nightly serenade as he was enshrouded by the cool, damp balminess of the late spring night.

The ghost pains of his lost arm were once again making him uncomfortable, sometimes with sharp, jabbing pains or just a dull ache. He was too heartbroken to be hungry, but the fire was comforting in the darkness. A cup of coffee was soothing. It was going to be another long, lonely, depressing night. He felt like he was the last surviving person on earth, and that was frightening.

He sat staring into the fire, lost in melancholy thoughts, when he heard a soft whine and looked up to see the old family collie dog, half starved, come limping hesitantly up to him. What a welcome sight! He was the first sign of life in this God-forsaken, desecrated shrine of desolation. After much petting, tears, and face licking, the two of them lay down beside the dying embers of the fire to try to sleep.

Jonathan lay awake thinking about the old dog. He knew he must be over fifteen years old now. He had gotten him for Johnny Boy's tenth birthday. They had other dogs, but the old collie was a special gift. Johnny Boy had fallen out of a tree and broken his leg earlier that summer, and he had had a hard time adjusting to his confinement.

Jonathan had found the pup in town at the livery stable. He knew the pup would be good to help Johnny Boy while away the hot summer days of recuperation. It was love at first sight between them, and from that day on both boy and dog were inseparable. Jonathan remembered that the old dog had moped around for days when Johnny Boy had gone off to the university. Johnny Boy had named him Major after a Major Stevens of the Revolutionary War whom he had read about in the history books and admired, partly because they both had the same last name.

"Father. Father. Help me!"

Jonathan looked around but could see nothing in the dark. Johnny Boy's voice again cried out from the darkness. Jonathan got up and began to search, hardly able to believe his ears. Johnny Boy was dead. How could he be calling him?

"Father, please, I can't move. I've been shot, Father. I need you!"

The voice had come from the direction of the river bottom. Jonathan began to stumble his way through the dark toward the river.

"Hurry, Father!"

Jonathan began to run, tripping over roots and vines and crying out, "Hang on, Johnny Boy. I'm coming!"

Weaker and more distant now, Johnny Boy cried out again for help. Faster and faster Jonathan stumbled through the dark. Finally he awoke in a cold sweat to discover the old collie dog licking his face and whining softly to comfort him.

Once again Jonathan knew he had been victimized by one of his many nightmares of the war. He hated the coming of night just because of those dreams with their varying dark clouds of melancholia. The old dog nuzzled down beside him in an effort to bring comfort, and Jonathan threw his arm around his neck and wept while listening to the distant squall of a wildcat down in the swamp.

At first light Jonathan awoke tired and disoriented. Then, flooded with the sights and memories of the night before, he got up and began to rebuild the fire. Breakfast consisted of a cup of strong coffee and the last of his army rations, which he shared with the dog, Major.

He sat pondering what he should do first. Food was a top priority, so he got up, found a broken-handled shovel, and headed for where the garden plot had been. Just maybe there would still be a few carrots, onions, and other vegetables left over from last fall's harvest. He would give anything just for something fresh to eat.

He thought about how his former slaves Sam and Eli had kept this garden. No one ever found a weed in their garden. He used to kid them about wearing the soil out in their search for weeds.

He looked out beyond the lawn areas and visualized the vast rolling hills and bottomlands where they had raised sugarcane, tobacco, rye, corn, wheat, and cotton. The cotton fields, with seventy slaves singing as they chopped or picked the cotton, the men stripped to their waists, the women in long, homespun, shapeless dresses. They provided the raw manpower that had made Castlemont a great self-sustaining plantation.

Jonathan could still remember how in the wintertime, the slaves had cut and hauled logs from the swamps to make lumber in his sawmill. They also had gathered pitch and made turpentine. He remembered the rich aroma of cured hams and bacon. He could almost taste them now along with the turkeys and chickens, all from the smokehouse. He felt like he could almost even hear the roosters crowing from the poultry sheds to announce the dawn of another new day. But all that was gone now, destroyed forever.

He was not sure when his overseer or Amelia had left the plantation, but he suddenly became aware that some of the nearby fields looked like they had been worked in the past year. Some even looked like they had been planted this spring, which made him think that there must be some of his slaves still about. At the same time, he feared it might be the work of squatters.

He next took the broken shovel and began to sift through the ashes of the big house, where he found a battered pot that he would be able to clean up and use. His mind languished over the great events of the past.

A man never forgot his roots. The values and standards had been bred into him for generations. He had been taught to be proud of his heritage. His great-grandfather had established Castlemont and had planted the live oak trees that now stood as weeping pallbearers at the funeral of the big mansion. His grandfather had built the mansion and named it after their family heritage in Scotland. His father, two uncles, and an aunt had all been born there. He, his brother, and his sister—both of whom had died of the "fever of '27"—as well as Johnny Boy and Georgiana, had all been born there.

Jonathan then remembered the family cemetery on the hill overlooking the beautiful, tranquil Altamaha River and hurried there to check it out. Once again his anger reached its zenith when he discovered the grave stones broken and strewn about. *I can't believe that the Yankees were such barbarians as to destroy a graveyard.* A feeling of utter desolation again swept over him. *Not only is my plantation gone, God has also forsaken me and left me without hope for anything. I must have done something terrible to deserve this.*

"Where are you, God?" he shouted out as he searched the sky now shrouded with dark, foreboding clouds. "I hate you for what you have done to me! I tried to live a good life, I have even prayed, but you probably never even heard me."

Jonathan was becoming accustomed to the taste of

bitterness that rose in his throat. The old dog quietly trudged along behind him.

Night finally came, and he again could not sleep. He stared into the darkness, watching the fireflies dancing across the yard as he reviewed the many times God had forsaken him. *God! I thought that you were either trying to teach me something or trying to strengthen my faith for something, that all these painful experiences were for my good and would work out best for me. I relied on that Bible verse that says, "All things work together for good for those who loved God" (Rom. 8:28). Well, I tried to love you, but things have not worked out for my good. Look at me now! I guess I must not have loved you enough. Like when Johnny Boy was killed, where were you? Any fool can see you have forsaken me. Why? What have I done to deserve this? Have I sinned so badly that I deserve this? I can't figure it out, but I know this much—there's no need to pray anymore or to even hope for anything.*

It was then that the volcano of anger and frustration erupted, and he sat down and wept like a baby until no tears were left.

The old collie dog seemed to understand his grief and laid his head on Jonathan's knee in an act of sad companionship and comfort. The warm breeze brushed away the ever-present mosquitoes and flies of summer, and Jonathan slept as the old dog stood guard over him.

The morning sun broke through the trees as the gentle breeze rustled the leaves, awakening Jonathan. He was surprised that he had fallen asleep and had slept through the night, but he had reached the point of total physical and emotional exhaustion. He could hear several crows making a ruckus down by the river and noticed a few honeybees hovering around some wild iris and honeysuckle that had survived the fire. The jays and mockingbirds were quarreling nearby over their territorial tree as a field mouse scurried through the grass.

Jonathan stood up to look around, and his nose caught the faint aroma of fresh smoke. Quickly he surveyed the area, thinking it might be army deserters, turned outlaws, or carpetbaggers, or maybe, if lucky, some of his slaves. His slaves! He didn't have slaves anymore, thanks to Abraham Lincoln.

His eyes caught a glimpse of the smoke down in the swampland near the river where he knew the slaves had hidden the horses. His hopes began to soar. Could it really be possible that some of the horses had been spared? He ran to saddle his horse and get his gun, almost afraid to even hope. He had had all the disappointments he could handle for a while.

Cautiously, taking his army-issue 44-caliber pistol in his left hand, he followed the trail through the brush in the general direction of where he had seen the smoke. Having been right handed, using a pistol now with his left hand was still awkward for him. Trying to carry his pistol and the horse's reins in the same hand was even more difficult. He had partially solved that problem by teaching his horse to be guided by knee pressure.

The horse suddenly stopped with his head and ears pointing straight ahead. Quietly Jonathan heard a familiar raspy, whispered voice say, "Mastuh Stevens, is dat youse?"

Quickly searching the brush, Jonathan finally made

out the faces of his old slave Ben, Ben's son, Asa, and Toby, his butler and valet. Their countenances were covered with fear. They looked like three ravaged men from the dungeons of jolly ole England, from where Jonathan's great grandfather had escaped to come to America. It was a wonder they even recognized Jonathan because of all the weight he had lost and the fact that he hadn't shaved for months.

The four men stood looking at each other, too overcome emotionally to even speak. All were so glad to see each other yet afraid to break the silence for fear the other might vanish. Finally the old dog barked and wagged his tail. That seemed to be the signal, and they all began to talk at once. Jonathan dismounted before the hesitant and puzzled men who politely looked away, being uncomfortable at seeing the clumsiness of their master without an arm.

They all in turn wept as they retold the terror of the Yankee invasion of Castlemont eight months before. They had fled into the swamp, fearing the worst from the invading hoard of Yankee soldiers. Some of the men had been beaten, and a number of the women had been raped by the soldiers. They did not know just how many slaves were still in the area. They had been too afraid to venture very far, but they did know that all the horses were safe. They had no way of even knowing that the war was over, nor did they know that they had been freed.

There was little talk among them as they returned with Jonathan to his campsite; each was lost in his own private thoughts. None seemed to be able to deal with their new relationship with Jonathan. No longer was it "master" and "slave." Nor was it "employer" and "employee." The future was unknown, and a new way had to be found.

Evening began to fall, and the three former slaves suddenly became aware that they needed to return to their families, who would be wondering where they were. Just then the old dog spotted a possum emerging from the edge of the brush, and the chase was on with the dog, Ben, and Asa in hot pursuit. Possum meant meat for supper to them, and they were not going to let "dat ole pos'um get away." Toby picked up the battered pot, which Jonathan had found in the ashes, and he was surprised they had missed it in their earlier search. He straightened the pan out the best he could and went to the pond to clean it up. He then stopped at the garden site and found a few scattered vegetables for a possum stew. Of course they would have to get some vegetables from their own little individual spring gardens hidden here and there throughout the lowlands near their hiding places and let their families know Jonathan had returned but needed rest and quiet.

Before long Ben and Asa returned to the campsite with the possum dressed out and ready for roasting on the open fire or to be made into stew. Jonathan had a major decision to make. He was really hungry, but eating possum was unthinkable to him. That was "nigger food." Only "darkies" ate possum. Army food and what they had been fed in the hospital was bad enough, but possum— never!

He thought of all the wonderful dinner parties that had taken place at Castlemont. They had been served on the lawns, on the veranda, or in the "great dining room," with the long table that would seat forty people. There were always slabs of barbecued roast beef and pork, roast turkey, goose or duck, and fish, with mountains of yams, potatoes, vegetables, and salads. There were also fine imported wines, teas, and coffees, followed by the delicate pastries. His father had hired a famous French chef to teach the kitchen staff the real art of food preparation. He remembered how the Negroes had huddled over the tables, dressed in their starched and pressed uniforms, serving and seeing to everyone's needs. His anger flared because he was beginning to realize that the loss of his wealthy lifestyle and his slaves left his future very uncertain. It was over. It would never be the same again.

Ben, Asa, and Toby were laughing and joking around the campfire, and the tantalizing aroma of the possum stew whetted Jonathan's appetite. He had talked Toby into cooking his portion separate from the possum by keeping a few vegetables separate. He knew that tomorrow they would have to catch some fish or kill several of the ducks that were on the pond. He could not bring himself to eat possum—yet.

After their dinner they began to make plans for their immediate future. The men decided that they would spend the night with Jonathan instead of returning to their own families.

"Toby, tell me all about the plantation. Where is my foreman, Alexander?"

"Mastuh Al'andar, he done lef' soon after you do, Mastuh Stevens. He say he go'en to war too. We darkies, we don' kno' what to do, so we jus' stay har an do as we al'ays do."

Ben and Asa nodded their heads in agreement. Jonathan was amazed.

"Who was in charge? Did you harvest the crops, and what did you do with them?"

"We's done de harvest, and Mastuh Barnes at de bank, he done sol' de crops, Mastuh Stevens, and puts de money in de bank for youse. But I har'd de bank, she gots burned down so's I don' kno' what's com' of de money. We'uns jus do de work, dats all we kno's to do, ex'cep' wait for youse. We's so' glad youse is here, Mastuh Stevens."

"Where are Mammy Lou and the rest of the women?"

"Oh da's is here and dar in 'r little places we'uns got. They be fine. Jus'a waitin' for us'n ta bring ya aroun or com' get 'em."

"Do any of you know anything about Amelia and Georgiana?"

"We'uns don' know nothin.' All we'uns knows is dat yo'r wife was ago'in to 'lanta."

Finally Jonathan said, "We need to find out just how many people are still in the area." They knew some might be hiding out somewhere in the river bottom and swamps. Ben thought of the dinner bell that had been used to call the slaves in from the fields for so many years. Since it was already dark, they decided to wait for daylight to begin their search for the bell.

The next morning they all began to search the area. They tramped through the weeds, tall grass, and surrounding brush, all to no avail. Returning to their campsite in discouragement, they decided to search along the edge of the pond, and to their amazement they caught a bright reflection of the sun in the deep water. Asa dove into the water and came up shouting, "T's de bell. She down nar a'right." They quickly got Jonathan's horse, and someone found a length of rope that they could use. With some great effort they extracted the bell from its watery grave.

Having forgotten all about eating, they spent the afternoon mounting the bell onto a makeshift platform. At the usual quitting time, Jonathan began to ring the bell hoping all the slaves would hear it and come in as they had been accustomed to doing in earlier, happier times. They waited, and their anticipation turned to silent discouragement as there was no response, even though they had sent word their master was back home to stay.

Night had fallen as the four sat around the campfire lost in their own thoughts. Finally Ben began to sing, and Asa quickly joined in, with Toby accompanying them with his old mouth harp. In a little while they began to hear singing from the surrounding darkness. Again they rang the bell and sang more fervently, with Jonathan even joining in with them. One by one faces began to appear on the fringes of the darkness, followed by shouts of, "Praise de Lawd! Mastuh Stevens is h're at las'! He's done com' home at las'!"

Mammy Lou came running up and threw her arms around Jonathan, shouting, "Praise de Lawd! Praise de Lawd! Mastuh Stevens, youse done come home to us po'r niggers. We'uns thought youse was dead. Oh, praise de Lawd!"

It was then that Mammy Lou noticed Jonathan was missing an arm. "Oh, Mastuh Stevens, what did they do to youse? Oh, youse po'r man. Youse just let ole Mammy Lou take care of youse. I's don't know whar Amelia is. She went off to Miss Georgiana's home in 'lanta, but we never h'ard no mo.'"

Mammy Lou had been Amelia's mammy, or nanny, having taken care of her when she was a little girl growing up and then caring for Johnny Boy and Georgiana. She was like family. Toby and Mammy Lou were husband and wife and had been house slaves, never having worked in the fields.

There was a great commotion with everyone singing, shouting, and dancing all at once around the fire. Jonathan stood speechless with tears flowing unchecked down his cheeks. He had not realized how lonely and lost he had been. He was amazed that these now ex-slaves had been such a vital part of his personal life and so loyal. Some of them had brought food with them, and this time Jonathan did not question its origin. He ate because he was famished. He was overwhelmed with the thought that these people actually loved him and had waited for him to return.

The hour grew late, and the people began to drift back to their own hiding places and beds, promising to return in the morning. The three men gathered their bedrolls and lay down beside the dying embers of the campfire with Jonathan. The old dog, Major, lay down next to Jonathan and placed his head in his lap.

The first thing the next morning, Jonathan asked Toby to give him a shave and haircut, so Toby went to his little home and got his razor and scissors, which he had found among the ashes of the mansion. Jonathan had still not mastered shaving with his left hand using a straight-edged razor. He then went over to the pond and took a bath the best he could. During the day, more and more people began to drift in from their distant hiding places. Mammy Lou arrived and demanded that Jonathan give her his clothes for a much-needed washing. While Jonathan was wrapped in a blanket, he and the men began to make some basic plans for the near future.

Atlanta Falls

Four months after Sherman's armies had destroyed Castlemont, they were now bogged down and would be for the next two months on the outskirts of Atlanta by the strongly entrenched Confederate army. The Confederate General Hood had ordered miles of trenches and bunkers dug to surround the city as a last-ditch effort to stop the "Mad Butcher." Atlanta was the hub of the whole transportation system in the South. The major munitions plants, hospitals, rolling mills for the making of weapons, and communications center were there. To lose Atlanta would be to finally lose the war. The Confederacy's back would be broken. There had been sporadic cannon fire and skirmishes during this time as the armies jockeyed for position and sized each other up. The newspapers had been filled with challenges and countercharges made by both armies.

Some said Sherman had asked Governor Brown to withdraw Georgia's troops from the Confederacy and save Atlanta and Georgia from the final destruction of the South. Jefferson Davis was set on fighting the Union armies till the last man fell.

The South was gradually having to admit the inevitable: "the cause was lost," and it was a bitter pill to swallow. They had been so sure that victory was theirs with "just one more battle." Nerves were frayed from the exhausting tension of the long, drawn-out four years of war. The deprivations, hunger, and losses of husbands, fathers, sons, and lovers, not to mention homes and lifestyles, had cut their hearts out.

The growing mass of wounded that poured into Atlanta every day required that every home become a hospital, which the army commandeered to provide a shelter for them. The multitude of refugees pouring in from the west with haunting stories of heavy losses of both Confederate and Yankee troops heightened the tension. Yet for every Yankee soldier killed or wounded, there seemed to be ten to take his place.

The news that the unconquerable General "Old Joe" Johnston had failed to stop the Yankee invasion from the west brought panic to the hearts of many. At last, even the state militia and the home guard, made up of the grandfathers, young boys, and ne'er-do-wells, known as "Governor Brown's Darlings," were called out to protect the bridges and entrenchments because there were just no more "regulars" for replacements. Ammunition, weapons, food, and medicine were all hard to come by.

The Confederate soldiers had reached a point of total exhaustion and were now fighting on raw nerve and cherished dreams alone. Reports of great acts of heroism, as well as those of desertions, trickled in. The famous Confederate yell had become more like a sullen whimper. Finally Sherman had waited long enough. He had no recourse but to warn the people to evacuate the city before he cut off the last of the supply lines into the city and the exits out of the city and began a full-scaled attack. Yet the people were reluctant to leave. Where would they go? Atlanta was sacred, the last stronghold of Georgia, and Georgia was the South. To many the fear of the unknown was greater than the fear of battle, or so they thought. People cowered in their homes with the fantasy that it would all pass over them. Jefferson Davis tried over and over to muster new hope and pride to fight on to victory, but the cause was already lost.

It had rained hard for three days and nights, and the morning of July 22, 1864, dawned to be a hot and sultry day. Sherman's forces were focused on the Ezra Church area west of the city, and the battle began with a full-scale bombardment of cannon fire raining indiscriminately upon the city.

The early dawn was ablaze with flashes of cannon fire and burning buildings. Soon a depressing cloud of gun smoke hovered over the city. Three divisions of Confederate soldiers were on a suicide mission to stop Sherman's forces, but they soon discovered the futility of it and quickly began to fall back and scatter.

Amelia awoke to the resounding scream of cannon fire and knew immediately that Atlanta was finally under full attack. Throwing off her covers and grabbing up her robe, she quickly descended the stairs and narrowly missed being hit by a cannon ball that crashed into her just-departed bedroom.

Georgiana came screaming from her room, and the two women fell into each other's arms. Mollie, the servant girl, came running hysterically from the kitchen, while Sarah, the cook, sat huddled in the kitchen beside the stove, swaying back and forth in a sort of a stupor, murmuring prayers. Jacob came rushing in the back door from the stables, so Amelia took time to quiet everyone down and explain exactly what they had to do so that they could leave the city within a few minutes.

Amelia ordered Jacob to hurry and bring about their carriage and wagon, which they had previously loaded with their household treasures. They had earlier decided not to "refuge" to Macon as many had done. Instead they planned to go to Georgiana's husband's family in Birmingham.

Amelia and Georgiana could hear the continuation of the retreating Confederate army, which was leaving the city to fend for itself. Huge explosions and balls of fire filled the air as the retreating army blew up the munitions plants and stockpiles of surplus supplies. They destroyed everything that they could not carry with them to keep the Yankees from getting them.

People in the streets fought over the supplies they had looted from some of those supply warehouses. The whole city was in cannibalistic turmoil and confusion as it became every man for himself. Even drunkenness and debauchery soon prevailed in every form as a result of people breaking into stockpiles of liquor at the two breweries.

The streets and roads soon became a quagmire of potholes and ruts due to the heavy rains that had fallen for the past three days. The clogged streets became crowded with the wounded and dying and vehicles of every description. Many vehicles were stuck in the mud, and others mired as they tried to get past. Frantically people tried to commandeer each others' horses or wagons, only to be fought off by whip or weapon.

Some people wandered about in a complete daze, seemingly oblivious to what was happening about them. There were those who were determined to stay by their properties and die, if necessary, to keep what belonged to them. Of course there were always the opportunists who were going about looting whatever they could find.

Smoke from the constant cannon fire and the burning city hung like a suffocating blanket of judgment over the city. Atlanta was suffering its own form of Sodom and Gomorrah.

Amelia drove one of their wagons, and Jacob drove the carriage through side streets, alleys, and across yards, dodging traffic and craters made by the ever-present cannon balls. She was glad she remembered to bring Jonathan's guns because on several occasions she had to fire warning shots at the hoodlums who tried to climb aboard or steal their horses.

There were hysterical people pushing and shoving their way through the crowd to escape the "wolves of chaos" snapping at their heels. At times when the procession came to a complete standstill because of an accident, Amelia or Jacob would get down and help clear away the wreckage while the other stood guard over their possessions. Amelia often called out words of encouragement to the disheartened and on several occasions shared some of their precious supply of water with a mother of a crying baby.

Night was fully upon them when they finally escaped the city and reached the Chattahouchee River, where they pulled their wagons under a giant gnarled oak tree and prepared for a sleepless night. Other people were making their camps under nearby trees as well. The nerve-racking din of exhausted mothers and frightened, tired, and hungry children filled the area. People argued over the best campsites, scraps of wood, and the best grass for their animals. Others called out the names of their separated or lost loved ones.

Jacob took the horses to the river to drink and then staked them out beside their wagons to feed on the trampled grass. Amelia and he stood guard while Georgiana, with the help of Sarah and Mollie, set up the camp and fixed the evening meal. It was very late when the camp gradually quieted down for the night, to be disturbed occasionally by crying mothers and children. Occasionally a dog growled or barked to disturb the quiet.

Amelia's and Georgiana's thoughts were centered upon the welfare of their husbands whose whereabouts were unknown. They knew Johnny Boy had been killed, but both wondered if their husbands were still alive and how they would ever find them. They talked little, afraid to voice their hopes and fears.

"Will it ever end?" Amelia sighed, speaking to no one in particular.

Jacob, Sarah, and Mollie hung their heads and stared into the fire. Georgiana dabbed at her eyes with a handkerchief and said, "The Lord only knows, Momma. I am so tired of this war and all of its miseries and uncertainties. You can't plan on anything or even hope."

Someone in the distance began playing a mournful tune on a mouth harp. It began to rain again to add to their final misery as they settled down for what remained of a sleepless night.

The next day Amelia encouraged their little troupe on its exhausting way. "It has been a long time since I have prayed, but I think we need to start the rest of our journey with a prayer."

Everyone paused and bowed their heads, and Amelia asked Sarah to say a prayer.

"Lawd, youse knows we'uns is scart and lost, an we'uns needs youse to lead us an pro'tex us on arn way. We'uns be thank'en youse for yor'n help. Amen."

The days became endless with many frustrating delays. Tempers flared, nerves fell apart, and fights erupted over broken down equipment, missing children, injured horses blocking the roads, and people crowding for space in the line or stopping to rest their animals. The traumatized troupe of refugees moved at a snail's pace. They had been on the road four days when one of the carriage wheels broke. This meant leaving the carriage behind with some of the less-important household items. In frustration the women broke down and wept.

"I just can't go on, Momma! I can't stand any more disappointments," cried Georgiana.

Amelia consoled her with a knowing hug and helped her into the remaining wagon. They drove away as looters piled onto the remains of the broken carriage like a bunch of vultures.

Food was fast running out, and they still had a long way to go. On the fifth day, Sarah came down with a high fever that meant further delays. On the evening of their eighth day, Mollie fixed gruel from the last of their food supply. Jacob had spent hours scouring the countryside looking for food, but so had all the other refugees. He had seen several fights over a possum or a squirrel. The local landowners were standing guard over their properties to prevent further looting.

Disheartened, they ate their final meal as they discussed their plight.

"I don't know what we are going to do, but we have to keep going. If all else fails, we can make some sort of tea out of grass and leaves that will keep us from starving," said Amelia.

They knew they had several days of travel before they would reach Birmingham. Sarah was somewhat better but was still too weak to sit up for any length of time.

They were in a desperate situation with no way to go but straight ahead. They had no idea of what they would find when they reached Birmingham. They even gave considerable thought to killing one of the horses for food, but also knew that would only slow their progress even more, and on the sixth night out someone stole their carriage horses. Each day that they traveled, they kept a sharp eye open for anything that might be edible. Amelia shot an evening dove and was glad that Jonathan had taught her the fine art of using a gun. They cooked the dove with some "poke-sally" greens and wild onions. Sarah got the larger portion of the broth, while the others just drank more water to fill up the empty spaces after their meager share had been eaten. Jacob was able to catch some fish at several of their stops, which helped tide them over.

On the evening of the eleventh day, they finally arrived in Birmingham and were welcomed by James' family, who graciously took them in and fed them the best they could out of their own meager rations.

Since the communication and supply lines had been disrupted into Birmingham, the Stewarts lived a quiet life throughout the remaining part of the war. The longer it lasted, less and less money was available for parties and other social functions, so the church became the social event of the community. The most important issues were food and shelter.

There were food shortages everywhere in the South, but it was felt the worst in the cities. Fortunately, at the beginning of the war, Mr. Stewart had dug up their expansive backyard and planted it to garden as part of the war effort. Without the garden, they would not have had any food for themselves. As it was, there was no flour, sugar, or coffee, except what they could buy on the black market at exorbitant prices.

Flour was selling for one hundred dollars a sack, if you could get it, with or without weevils. They had not had any meat for months. Dogs, cats, and even rats had disappeared from the city streets. Now for the Stewarts it would be a greater struggle with five additional mouths to feed.

During the next few days, Amelia and Georgiana sorted through all their belongings that they had saved to see what of value they might sell to help buy food. There were many tears as they shared memories over each item. Confederate money was now worthless, and the barter system alone was in use. First, they sold the horses for some of their basic needs, which helped out for a few days. Finally Amelia had to trade her precious matching diamond necklace and earrings for half a sack of flour. Her diamond dinner ring was traded for about twenty-five pounds of meat of questionable origin. Jonathan had given them to her on their tenth wedding anniversary. The meat proved to be so tough they had to boil most of it in order to even eat it.

Their future looked very bleak, and Amelia worried about being a burden on the Stewarts. Georgiana began immediately seeking some kind of employment to help. Even if she had to be paid in food, it would help.

There had been no word from either Jonathan or James. They also missed Johnny Boy. He had been such a fine boy and the only male to carry on the Stevens' name. Amelia remembered how proud she had been to present Jonathan with a fine son and future heir of Castlemont.

She knew that somehow she had to get back to Castlemont, but that was now over three hundred miles away. The only possible way would be by team and buggy, and that was not safe. It might as well have been in a different world.

The Traitor

Jonathan had been back at Castlemont two weeks when one night someone heralded the camp.

"Hello, the camp! Hello, the camp! Can I come in and sit a spell?"

At first Jonathan thought he was having another of his frequent nightmares. Then the old dog barked and Toby hollered, "Who dat?"

"Name's Barker! William Joseph Barker. Most folks call me Billy Joe."

Jonathan had grabbed up his pistol, and both Ben and Asa had crawled out of the light of the fire.

"Well, Billy Joe, come on in if you are alone."

Toby sat staring into the darkness.

Jonathan was absolutely flabbergasted that a Yankee soldier would have the audacity to come into a Southern camp of Confederates. The war might be over, but it was not forgotten. Yankees were not welcome even though there were occupation troops throughout Georgia. Therefore, taking no chances, he kept his pistol pointed at the Yankee intruder.

Sensing Jonathan's anger, Billy Joe held up his hands and called out, "Sir, let me explain who I am and why I am here."

Tensions were high, and Billy Joe realized that both Ben and Asa had materialized out of the dark on each side of him armed with clubs.

"Mister, you had better talk fast and straight," Jonathan said.

"Sir, can I lower my hands and talk as one gentleman to another?"

Jonathan's heritage intervened, and he extended the courtesy, murmuring grudgingly, "No Yankee is a gentleman."

"Sir, I was born and partially reared in Youngstown, Ohio. My parents died when I was still just a boy, so I was sent to live with my uncle, on my mother's side, in Mobile, Alabama, where I grew up. My uncle was one of the outstanding lawyers in that area, name of Stollings. I went to the university, studied law, and then practiced law for five years in my uncle's law firm before the war started. I was really torn as to what to do about the war, but my uncle encouraged me to join the Union army because he believed that the hope of all the states of our great nation was to be found in preserving the constitution and by-laws of our total nation.

"He and I both realized that it would pose a special hardship upon the slave owners of the South, but in the long run, all would benefit. My uncle sold his law practice shortly before he died, and I have no practice to return to. So, sir, I decided to return to the South anyway because I feel this is where my true roots are. I know there are many who want to continue to ravage the South even worse than what has already happened. The South will need good lawyers who have experienced both sides of the issue for this transition period."

"Billy Joe Barker, you are a traitor! You betrayed the South by joining up with the Yankees! You killed my son! Destroyed my plantation! You took away my slaves and my right arm, and you expect me to sit here and listen to your poppycock talk about reconstruction of the South!" His voice kept escalating, louder and louder, as he became more agitated. "I have a mind to shoot you right here and now. To me the war will never be over!" With that, Jonathan raised his gun.

Ben hollered, "Wait, Mastuh! He no done all do's ter'ible t'ings he'self. Ta war's over."

There was a long, tense silence with nobody moving. Hostility filled the air, waiting for a mighty explosion.

Finally Jonathan seemed to wilt and said, "I only wish it were true."

Billy Joe said, "Sir, our hardest battles are yet to come. The reconstruction of the South will not be an easy task, and it will take years to complete, if ever."

"Just what do you have in mind for the South, Mr. Billy Joe Barker?" sneered Jonathan.

"Better representation in congress, reconstruction of the economy, diversification of industry and farming, education of the freedmen, and new laws to match the changing times."

"That's a big order," said Jonathan. "Just how do you propose to do all of that?"

"It will require involvement of every landowner and

taxpayer in the South. We Southerners have been used to living our own lifestyle, which lifted up our traditions. Now we have to change our vision and attitudes and get involved where the action is, in the challenges of economic competition and industry of our whole nation. We have to learn new methods of farming, crop rotation, and marketing. You have two choices as I see it, sir. One is to let the land be taken over by opportunistic carpetbaggers who are already exploiting the South, or you can do something that is mentioned in the Bible."

Jonathan exploded. "What has the Bible got to do with the war and the South, or anything else?"

Billy Joe went on to explain, "There is a story in the Bible where the landowner selected his most faithful servants and divided his land up among them to be farmed according to his directions and their abilities. That way they had a sense of belonging, and they worked hard for both themselves and their master. Your former slaves who have remained here on your land have worked your land for years, sir. They probably know it even better than you do, and they have proven themselves worthy by standing by you while you were away at war, even though they did not get paid for it. They had no way of knowing you were alive and would come home. By the way, sir, I don't know your name."

"Name's Stevens, Jonathan Stevens."

Grudgingly Jonathan consented to listen and put away his gun. They talked long into the night, exchanging their views on various subjects until exhaustion forced them all to lie down to sleep beside the dying fire.

The next day was Sunday. Billy Joe had explained the

night before that his parents had been devout members of the Methodist Episcopal Church in Ohio, but his uncle and aunt had been strong, "hard-shell" Baptists. Therefore, he had been raised in the Baptist church and taught to observe Sunday as a day of worship and rest. He asked Jonathan if he would like to join with him in reading from the Bible. Jonathan indifferently agreed to listen, and they set the time for following the evening meal, when the Negroes would all be gathered around.

Before the war, Jonathan and Amelia had been members of the Anglican church. Jonathan had attended fairly regularly to please Amelia and to socialize with their friends and neighbors. Religion was something he could take or leave alone. It made him no never mind. Jonathan questioned that if God was real, why did he allow the war and Johnny Boy's death?

He was now confronted with a new monster in his life—his peace with God. Was God real? He had so many unanswered questions, and he was afraid of what some of those answers might be. He was afraid of this Yankee because of his religion and abolitionist ideas.

The morning was spent working to further improve their campsite and searching for food. Billy Joe had ventured down toward the river and was fortunate enough to shoot a young buck that somehow had been missed by the Yankees. Toby supervised the preparations for the evening barbecue of roast venison as more and more of the darkies began to assemble. Most of them had small spring gardens hidden away throughout the swamplands and brought food to be shared.

It was a festive time for the Negroes. The war was

finally over, and their master had returned. Everyone was so relieved that they had survived to see another day, and with the master home, everything would be all right. They would now begin to put their lives together with Jonathan leading them.

Out of their meager provisions, each had sacrificially contributed something for the meal. The meat dishes consisted of the venison, possum, fish, and squirrel. Other dishes consisted of salad greens, onions, cornbread, hush puppies, a few spring potatoes, small carrots, and early English peas. It had been a beautiful, balmy day, with a light breeze blowing through the new leaves. The pungent aroma of new grass and the awakening earth filled the air.

All the food was carefully laid out on makeshift tables or on blankets on the ground. During the evening the children played games; there was singing, dancing, and storytelling, and yet a sense of calm. A new life was beginning, and everyone was excited except Jonathan.

A sudden hush fell over the festivities when a little boy stood before Jonathan and, looking up, said, "Mastuh Jon Jon, w'at hap'ened to yo'r a'm?"

Mammy Lou rushed over to grab up her grandson, but Jonathan waved her off, knelt down, picked him up with his good arm, and said, "What's your name, young man?"

"Benji."

"Well, Benji, I remember you were just a tiny baby when I went away to war, and now you are a big boy. You asked about my arm. Well, I got shot in the war, and the doctor had to take my arm off to save my life."

"Did it hu't, Mastuh Jon Jon?"

"Yes, Benji, it hurt real bad, but it couldn't be helped."

After the meal was over and the sun had set, everyone gathered about the large fire for the Bible reading. The Negroes began to sing their beloved spirituals. Someone had brought a fiddle; another had a mouth harp. Jonathan had secluded himself on the fringe of the crowd and quietly listened, with Benji sitting beside him. He withdrew into his own thoughts and feelings, more like an outsider than the master of Castlemont.

Billy Joe finally stood up with his well-worn Bible in hand. He began reading from the book of Genesis, beginning with the story of God calling Abraham to leave his homeland and start a new life (Gen. 12). Billy Joe expanded this thought to show how it applied to their lives.

"Abraham was an ordinary man who believed in God, who trusted God without hesitation. Therefore, God asked Abraham to do a special job for him—to start a new life in a new country, to become the leader of God's people so as to keep them from destroying themselves. You see, in the beginning God made man in his own image, or likeness, with the knowledge to choose right and wrong. He gave man dominion, or control, over all of his creation to use it as man chose. Man, in his greed, chose to misuse his powers of choice and tried to establish his own little kingdoms and forget about his relationship with God. That is why we have just fought this terrible war. God did not intervene in the war because of the people's sinfulness. The Bible says that 'if my people, who are called by my name, will humble themselves and pray and seek my face and turn from their wicked ways, then will I hear from heaven and will forgive their sin and will heal their land'" (II Chron. 7:14).

Billy Joe went on to say, "God has now placed us in a new country that offers new opportunities for everyone. All we have to do is follow God's leading, and our lives will be blessed far more than they had previously been in the past. It will require our willingness to give up our old selfish habits, traditions, and old ways of doing things, but everyone will be free. It will be hard, and it will take time. But it will be for the good of everyone, not just a privileged few as in the past. We just have to be willing to be patient and trust God. The way we overcome the past is to build for the future with God."

Jonathan was furious. *How dare this imposter tell me he had to give up everything he had believed in and owned? What does this Yankee traitor know about the real traditions of the South? He has not lost a thing because of the war. Traditions are sacred. They are unspoken law.* "Be patient and trust God to guide you!" *What nonsense. What has God ever done for me?*

Jonathan was challenged by Billy Joe's reference that "nothing was impossible with God." *I don't know what he means by following God's will or direction. Does he expect God to come right down here and tell me how to run my plantation? If there really is a God, I think he would be too busy to be worried about being a planter.*

Jonathan was not able to recognize that he was afraid of change. He was angry that he had even been asked to think about change. The South had always lived this way.

Yet he knew in his heart he had to change, and that made him even more frightened and angry. The future was out of his control, and Jonathan had always prided himself in his being in control.

Nothing would erase the fact that Johnny Boy was dead; that was a fact. The war had ruined him, and that was a fact. Billy Joe reminded Jonathan a lot of Johnny Boy. They both were about the same age, and their personalities and degree of intelligence were similar. They even looked somewhat alike. It was so frustrating and confusing; he wanted Johnny Boy to be right there with him.

Finally everyone gathered up their families and drifted off to their makeshift homes, leaving Jonathan and Billy Joe sitting around the fire. Jonathan wanted Amelia to be there with him. He missed her terribly and longed for her gentle sustaining touch and presence. He longed to hold her in his arms, kiss her gently, and tell her how much she meant to him.

He had sent a letter to let her know he was safe and coming back to Castlemont, but he had not been able get up enough nerve to mention in the letter that he had lost his arm. Maybe he felt that if she knew she wouldn't come back at all. Anyway, he anxiously looked for her each day.

The fire crackled and popped as each man sat lost in his own thoughts of the evening. Jonathan finally said, "You know, Billy Joe, a man needs his wife. A man just isn't complete without his wife beside him. Amelia was my whole life. Her smile and touch gave me life."

"I guess that is why the Bible says, 'God made woman to be a "help-meet" to her husband.'"

"Is that what the Bible says? I just wish Amelia would come back. I really miss her. It has been six months since I sent her a letter while I was still in the hospital and several weeks since I sent a letter from here, and we haven't heard a word."

"Mr. Stevens, I think you need to go to Atlanta and check on things. She may be waiting to hear from you, or she may have heard erroneously that you have been killed. Maybe she does not have the money or the way to travel so she could come back."

"Amelia is a wonderful wife. I always knew I could count on her support. Were you ever married? I haven't heard you mention a wife or a sweetheart that might be waiting for you."

"No, I never married. While I was in law school, I had a number of opportunities, and I might say a number of anxious mothers wanting their daughters to marry a promising young lawyer like myself. But my mind was centered on completing my education. Then as a young starving lawyer just starting out in practice, I was just too poor to afford a wife. Maybe I was too particular, and my standards were too high."

"What do you mean that your standards were too high?"

"Well, first of all, my wife will have to be of like faith in the Lord, with the same high principles I have set for myself. Secondly, she will have to be well educated with an open mind to new ideas and capable of making her own sound decisions. Thirdly, she will need to be a dedicated homemaker and mother. Lastly, she will have to be the very person I feel God has chosen for me."

"That is a tall order, Billy Joe, but this thing about God choosing a wife for you, how are you supposed to know that?"

"That is a hard answer to explain. God speaks to us in many ways and makes things happen in such a way that you just can't ignore. Sometimes he speaks to us through a Bible verse he brings to our minds. Sometimes he speaks through several other people. Sometimes he speaks to us while we are praying, and we just know because we know and have a great sense of peace. Take for instance my coming here to Castlemont. When the war was over, I was at loose ends not knowing just what to do or where to go. After praying about it, I felt I was to trust God, and so I got on my horse and started on my journey south. I had no set destination in mind except I wanted to do God's will for my life. At this point I am not positive whether I am to stay here with you indefinitely or to set up a law practice somewhere. When I arrived here at Castlemont, I somehow felt I had arrived at my destination for the time being. I believe this is where God wants me to be. This is a place where I feel I can be of help. Does that make any sense, Mr. Stevens?"

"Well, I don't know about God having any part in it. But you are here, and so far I have needed you to help me think things through and get organized with a definite sense of direction. We will just have to see how this all plays out."

"Now about me having a wife, I feel God will bring a good woman into my life, and both of us will know that we are the one that God has chosen for each other. Kind of like we will both be marching to the same drumbeat, so to speak." Billy Joe tossed another stick on the fire.

"Well, that was kind of the way it was for Amelia and me. The very first time I saw her, I knew I was going to do my best to marry her. She was the woman for me and always has been, and I don't want any other. She said the same thing about me, that is, before I lost my arm. Now I am not so sure."

"Well, Mr. Stevens, if Amelia loved you like you said she did, she will still love you without your arm."

"I hope so."

It grew late, and the men decided to turn in for the night. Billy Joe got up, yawned, and headed to bed as Jonathan banked the fire for the night.

Jonathan and Billy Joe continued their discussions around the evening camp fires for the next several weeks, getting better acquainted and more comfortable with each other.

"As I see it, Mr. Stevens, the major difference between the North and the South is cultural. The North is a composite of many ethnic groups who have a wide, diverse, industrial background. The South is basically agricultural and made up mainly of a minority of aristocratic plantation owners and merchants, basically of Scotch-Irish background, with a few English, French, and Spanish in the mix. This minority has controlled the destiny of thousands of slaves and those referred to as white trash. There is an upper class and a lower class, with a wide margin between them, and no real middle class."

"That may be true," said Jonathan, "but that is the way it is and always has been. Our heritage is very important to us, and we are not about to give it up without a struggle. We may have lost the war, but we still believe we were right."

"The major cause for the South losing the war was their lack of industrial diversification and population. Atlanta alone was the main industrial center for the whole South." Billy Joe went on to say, "The mines for raw materials, the major sea ports, and industrial cities are all in the North. The North is industrial, and the South is agricultural. Also there is the fact that the majority of our nation's population is in the northern states. The northern army was about ten times the size of the army of the South."

"I don't care about all of that. The North had no right to demand that the South give up our slaves. We have always had slaves, and you can't run a plantation without slaves. We should be able to have our 'states rights.'"

"Mr. Stevens, our United States Constitution was established to protect and preserve the rights of each state and each and every person who lives within them. That includes the Negro. Our government is designed to include all people by representation. The South has never recognized the human rights of the Negro. He has never been allowed an education, a voice in government, or a vote."

"That is because the nigger is not smart enough to know what is good for him."

"Has he ever been given a chance?" said Billy Joe.

"What you are talking now is a rebellion among the

niggers. We have to keep them under control for their own good."

"Does keeping them under control mean that it is all right to break up their families or beat them or rape their women?"

"I have never unnecessarily beaten my slaves, and I have never raped any of my female slaves."

"That may be true in your case, Mr. Stevens, but that does not speak for all plantation owners. You will have to agree that there are a large number of mulattos out there."

"Billy Joe, you can't force Northern morality upon the South. Just look at the ghettos in the Northern cities. Why, I have been told that it is not safe for a white man to be found on certain streets in parts of New York City or Chicago after dark. Do you want that for us here in the South?"

"You have a good point there, Mr. Stevens, but that does not make it right. Yet you must remember that even in the ghetto each person has the freedom of choice. He can go to school, work at a job of his choice, or live where he chooses. Most people in the ghettos of the North are there because first, they are among people of their own ethnic background. Second, because of their lack of education, they have to work at low paying jobs, and third, they are afraid to branch out on their own."

As the weeks went by, Jonathan and Billy Joe worked closely together concentrating on providing food for everyone. It was mid summer now, and everyone's private gardens were in their prime, which was a big help.

Jonathan would catch himself continually comparing

Billy Joe to Johnny Boy. Both had minds sensitive to the needs of others. Both were willing to try new ways to achieve a goal, and both were hard workers. Therefore, Jonathan became more and more attached to Billy Joe. He was like a second son, and that was comforting to him. They even argued just for the sake of arguing, which helped them see all sides of a given situation.

Billy Joe's keen reasoning powers always seemed to win out in the long run, and Jonathan finally had to admit to himself that he really needed him to help rebuild Castlemont to its eminent greatness under these new conditions. Jonathan even caught himself on several occasions calling Billy Joe "son." Slightly embarrassed, he would try to explain the slip by saying he was getting absentminded. He realized that he really wanted him to stay and would dread the day that he would feel the need to move on.

Maybe Billy Joe was really part of God's plan to take the place of Johnny Boy. He knew he was not prepared to run the plantation alone. He desperately needed someone he could count on since Amelia was not there, and since he did not have an overseer, there really was no one else to turn to. Billy Joe had many revolutionary ideas, and Jonathan knew many changes would be necessary to survive in the new South.

One night Jonathan and Billy Joe continued their discussion of the necessary changes.

"You know, Mr. Stevens, God never intended for any man to be a slave to another man. It was man's greedy nature that brought about slavery in the first place. God's Son, Jesus Christ, died on the cross so that all men—

black, white, yellow, red, or brown—could have an equal opportunity and be free. This whole war we have just fought was to free the Negroes of slavery and give them the same opportunities to develop their talents like any other man. Mr. Stevens, I have no other commitments, so if you will have me, I would like to stay right here at Castlemont and help you in leading Castlemont into becoming a leader in the emancipation of the Negro and the South."

Jonathan sat quietly for a long time lost in thought. He was in a state of confusion. Part of him was absolutely furious; the other part had a sense of guilt and humiliation, yet somehow a sense of peace. Finally he said, "What you are proposing is to get me hung from the nearest of these oak trees as an abolitionist. Everybody knows Negroes are cursed by God and have always been slaves, and that is not going to change overnight!"

"No, Mr. Stevens, God never cursed the Negro. The white man did that to try to excuse his own sinful greed. God curses man's sin, not the man. It is part of man's human nature to try to put others down into some form of servitude to him, so he can be a king and rule over everyone within his little kingdom. God's way is to lift men up, to help them to become better than they are now, to set them free of their greedy, sinful nature."

Jonathan again was quiet in thoughtful speculation. He finally said, "What are you proposing that we do?"

"The first thing we need to do is to stop referring to your former slaves in a derogatory way by calling them 'niggers, negroes, darkies, and slaves.' They are human beings just like we are and have names just like you and me, and they are now 'freedmen.' We need to refer to them individually by name or collectively as freedmen."

"But none of them have a last name, nor can they read or write. What are you going to do about that?"

"I suggest that we begin by letting them choose their own last name. Some of them may want the name of Stevens because they have been a part of your plantation family all of their lives. They are freedmen now and should be allowed to choose their own last name. Maybe some will want to even change their first names or nicknames. I hope that in time we can start a school and educate them."

"Now you are talking to get us hung as abolitionists," said Jonathan.

Several more weeks went by before Jonathan agreed to let the freedmen chose their own names. Of course, almost all of them could neither read nor write, so Billy Joe entered their new names into the new plantation ledger. Jonathan was astonished at how many wanted to have his last name. He had a very difficult time of breaking his habit of referring to them as "Negroes," "darkies," "niggers," or "slaves." But he tried hard because he wanted to be a leader in the reconstruction of the South, and as Billy Joe had said, "It has to start somewhere, and it might as well be with Castlemont."

Learning to treat the freedmen as fellow human beings took a lot more discipline and concentration on Jonathan's part, and word soon got out so that his neighbors began to criticize him for entertaining ideas about educating the Negroes, which would probably set himself up for a big uprising.

Jonathan was often shunned or berated as a "crazy nigger lover" when he went to Cedar Crossing for supplies and more than once was warned that he could expect a visit from the Ku Klux Klan. The Klan began to make its presence felt throughout the area on a regular basis, terrifying the freedmen and harassing many of the white people as they traveled the road to and from town.

As summer progressed they had gathered all of Jonathan's thoroughbred horses from the swampland and surveyed the outlying crops stored in sheds that had been overlooked by Sherman's army. Jonathan was proud of the loyalty his former slaves had shown by continuing to till some of the fields and to plant and harvest the best they could in his absence. The money they would receive from the sale of some of the horses and the crops would give them some much-needed working capital to get started on the reconstruction of Castlemont. Jonathan was very proud of his fine horses, especially Prince Royal, his famous stud who had sired ten fine foals while Jonathan was away at war. He felt very fortunate for having the horses and would have thanked God for their preservation if he and God had been on speaking terms.

There was a certain sense of security in knowing that there would at least be a small harvest and income. The cotton and tobacco growing in the fields now looked as if it would be of a high yield.

Jonathan was also proud that some of his former slaves had not run away when Amelia and Mr. Alexander left the plantation. The camp population had now reached fifty-seven freedmen who had continued to remain on the plantation property after Sherman's sweep. Mammy Lou took charge of organizing the families into their new settlement near where the former slave cabins had been.

Jonathan was thankful for Billy Joe's ability to carefully explain the meaning of their emancipation to them. To some of the younger ones, it was a time of rejoicing because they had high hopes and big expectations. They quickly departed into the night to seek their fortune in the cities, but later some of them returned disillusioned. To the older slaves it was a time of great sorrow and fear. Where could they go? What could they do? All they had ever known was to work for "Mastuh Stevens." None of them had ever seen a big city. They were also concerned about being cared for in their old age. Their mothers and fathers and some of their own children were buried in the slave cemetery at Castlemont, and that was where they wanted to be buried. They begged Jonathan to let them stay, offering to do anything.

Jonathan and Billy Joe took many long walks or rode their horses across the fields so they could talk about the situation. The freedmen had served him faithfully, and Jonathan did not want to desert them now by turning them out to fare for themselves. Yet he knew he could not keep them on as slaves. Secretly Jonathan was glad that Billy Joe had come along at just the right time to help him make these decisions. The young man had a good head on his shoulders. However, in no way was Jonathan ready to fully credit God for sending Billy Joe in his time of need. He and God were still not on speaking terms.

He wished Billy Joe didn't have this thing about religion. Religion was for women. *To me, the idea of God directing our lives is ridiculous. I don't think God, if there really is one, would have time for our personal wants.*

In the meantime, Billy Joe realized that for the first time in many years, he had found a real home. He was needed here, and he was able to make a major contribution. He liked Jonathan, who had many qualities he remembered his father having. He realized that God had a special purpose for his being at Castlemont, and that was exciting. He looked forward to each day with a sense of divine expectancy, and he spent special time in periods of praise and prayer so that he would be in tune with God's will.

In the back of his mind was an ideal that he had wanted to see put in practice for years in the South, the ideal where all men were treated as equals as the constitution stated they should be, where all people had the freedom to live and work where they wanted to and at what they wanted to do. It would be a place where an education was mandatory for everyone including the Negro, a place where wages were fair and equal to ability and effort, a place where the idea of the parable of the talents like what Joseph Davis successfully started in 1827 at the Davis Bend Freedmen's Colony south of Vicksburg on the Mississippi River.

Jonathan gradually was becoming more open to thoughts of change, and Billy Joe knew he would have to be careful in presenting too many new ideas that might go against the currents of traditions. He knew he must spend more time praying so God would give him guidance in timing and in the preparation of Jonathan to receive the new ideas.

The day finally came, and the timing seemed right, as Billy Joe and Jonathan were resting after dinner with their cups of coffee around the fire pit.

"Mr. Stevens, I have been doing a lot of thinking. As I have said before, my uncle and aunt have both passed away, and I don't really have any place to go or call home, and Castlemont just feels like home to me for the time being."

There was a very brief pause before Jonathan said, "I'm glad you feel that way, Billy Joe. You have come to mean a lot to me these past few weeks, and I have to admit I really need you, even if you are a Yankee and have all these modern newfangled ideas. I would like to have you stay and help me, as you can see I am in no shape yet to run this plantation alone. I always had an overseer, who actually ran the plantation for me, but I can't afford one now, nor can I afford to pay you."

"Mr. Stevens, I'm not talking about getting paid. I'm talking about us needing each other and doing what is right for Castlemont. We will work out the problems one at a time and make this a great success."

Daily Jonathan and Billy Joe continued to talk about the future of Castlemont as they rode their horses over the land. Gradually the pieces of the puzzle began to fall into place as they worked out their reconstruction plans. First and foremost, a sawmill was needed to make the lumber for all of the new buildings because Sherman's armies had destroyed all the sawmills in the area. Besides, that would be a new source of revenue for Castlemont and an opportunity for employment for some of the Negroes. They would need to sell off some of the horses to purchase the necessary equipment and hire an experienced millwright to run it. They had checked around to find out how much starting a sawmill would cost. It burned Jonathan to know that they would have to order it from Northern Yankees. The biggest obstacle was how to farm the plantation without the use of slaves. They decided that the freedmen who had stayed would harvest this year's crops and receive wages through the sale of the crops. It was hard for Jonathan to see how there could be any profit if he had to pay wages. In the past he had provided the Negroes with their basic needs of food and shelter, and they seemed happy.

After the sawmill was up and running and they had lumber to work with, they would begin to build all the necessary homes for everyone to live in, beginning with homes for the older residents.

Jonathan still had dreams of rebuilding the original Castlemont, and everything would be just the same as before. Amelia would come back. There would be big parties, with dancing in the grand ballroom and on the veranda. The fields would flourish with abundant crops. The buildings would be immaculate, and the yards and gardens would again be beautiful. He would be able to have his thoroughbred horses and take them to the races. He would be able to take Amelia to Europe on a second honeymoon. Georgiana would bring her children home for great extended visits. Everything would be the same, except for Johnny Boy of course. The reality of Johnny

Boy's death burst Jonathan's daydreaming and brought him back to the ugly presence of reality.

Gradually, Billy Joe introduced the idea of "shared responsibility" as taken from the parable of the talents found in the Bible (Mt. 25:14). At first Jonathan absolutely refused, saying, "It will never work!" It was like giving his plantation away. No Negro was smart enough to farm by himself, and he was not going to have anything to do with anything that had to do with the Bible. That was that! Quietly Billy Joe asked the question, "Mr. Stevens, who took care of the plantation the four years you were gone to war?"

Jonathan knew he was trapped in a corner.

"I don't care! No nigger is going to take over my plantation! It is my plantation, and I will do with it what I want! Castlemont has always been run by the Stevens family. It has been passed on from father to son and always will be!"

Jonathan suddenly realized he had no son and never again would have a real son to pass Castlemont down to, and he began to weep. Billy Joe sat quietly by, and the old dog flopped his tail on the ground as he lay watching his master once again pouring out his deep sorrow as he wept. In the distance, the soft melody of "Swing Lo, Sweet Chariot" came from someone's mouth harp.

In the following days, as they went about their work, Jonathan kept asking Billy Joe more about "that crazy story of yours."

"It all begins with having the right attitude. The landowner was a wise man, a good steward of everything he possessed, because he believed that everything of his really belonged to God, who had created all things. He knew that he was really just the caretaker for God and got to enjoy the benefits of it. He sought out the very best use of everything he owned because he knew in his heart that God had blessed him to use it wisely, and God allowed him to prosper because he did use it wisely. The owner not only believed in himself, he believed in his servants. He believed in their potential, their creativity, and their faithfulness. He wanted them to discover their own potential for themselves, and he was willing to take the risk to bring that about for them. He only knew he had nothing to lose but everything to gain in that he was developing the potential of those who worked for him, and through them, he too would benefit. It was a challenge for everyone involved. Did you ever hear of the Davis Bend Freedmen's colony, also known as the Community of Cooperation, which was south of Vicksburg?"

"It seems like I did hear something about a strange setup where Negroes worked on a plantation and headed up their own community, even had their own sheriff and court. The battle of Vicksburg took place just north of it."

"That is right, Mr. Stevens. Jefferson Davis' older brother Joseph started it, and it has been working successfully for almost forty years. That is kind of like what I am suggesting for Castlemont."

Jonathan continued to ponder these strange new ideas and one night asked Billy Joe to read the story to him from out of the Bible. As Billy Joe read, Jonathan kept murmuring to himself.

"It will never work in this day and age. That man

never had the same problems we are faced with now. It just won't work."

Billy Joe startled him by saying, "Mr. Stevens, it won't work if we don't try it."

Jonathan responded angrily, "We'll not talk about it anymore; it just won't work."

With that, they went to bed. Before dropping off to sleep, Billy Joe took time to have his usual time of worship in praise and adoration. He brought before God details of his life, his feelings for Jonathan and his concerns, his hopes, and his dreams.

Jonathan, on the other hand, tossed and turned throughout the night. His sleep was disturbed by dreams of the once beautiful Castlemont, now grown up in weeds and brush because there was no one to work the land. Once he saw himself frantically trying to harvest the endless fields of grain with a small hand sickle. Then he visualized a swarm of locusts descending on his crops, and he alone was feverishly running through the fields trying to drive them away. He then saw himself trying to pick the cotton by himself, with only one hand, and the cotton bag dragging defiantly behind him. The fields were endless, and the storm clouds were gathering. He knew he had to get the crop harvested before it was ruined, so he ran for help but could not find anyone who would help him.

He awoke in a panic, ready to run out through the night. He sat down on the side of his makeshift bed running his hand through his hair. The old dog came to him to be petted, and Jonathan thought, *You are my only true friend. You stand by me regardless of what is happening, and you make no demands of me.* Jonathan got up and went out to build up the fire and have a cup of coffee. What was he going to do with Billy Joe and his strange story? What was he going to do with Castlemont? Were things ever going to get back to normal? His loneliness cried out for Amelia, and he wished he would hear from her. He went back to bed and once again tried to sleep.

The New Arrivals

Jonathan woke with the old dog nuzzling his cheek and pulling at his shirtsleeve. The dog ran to the doorway of the dilapidated, make-shift tent, came back, looked at Jonathan, whined, ran back to the doorway, and looked out. Jonathan finally realized that the dog was trying to tell him something, so he got out of bed, grabbed up his pistol, and followed the dog to the doorway of the tent.

There was a full moon, and he immediately saw a strange-looking man sitting cross-legged beside the dying fire. Jonathan quietly crept closer and realized he was some kind of old Indian.

Without turning his head, the Indian said, "I am Wy Cha Nee Chi, which means, 'He Walks by Night.' I have returned to the place of my ancestors who once lived here many moons ago."

By this time, Billy Joe and Ben had arrived from their beds, swiftly followed by Toby and Asa. The old Indian went on to say, "I have come that I might die and be buried here in the land of my people."

Jonathan and Billy Joe looked at each other, each wondering if the Indian had weapons and if there were other Indians hidden nearby in the shadows of the night. After carefully looking around and listening to the crickets chirp, they shrugged their shoulders and sat down across the fire from the old Indian. Ben gathered up some wood and put it on the fire. As the blaze began to lighten up the surrounding area, they could see the old Indian had brought a freshly killed deer for the camp, his bow and arrows lying beside the carcass.

Soon the night began to fade with the dawning of the new day, and Wy Cha Nee Chi told them how he had received his name. Often as a child his mother would find him walking in the night, or sleepwalking. He was a member of the Creek tribe who had lived here and then been forced off their tribal lands. He went on to say that the Nune-hee had directed his paths to come back here to die.

Jonathan and Billy Joe had both heard of the legends of the Nune-hee, who was like a patron saint of the Indians, who guided the lost and injured.

"Listen, the Yunwee Chuns Dee are singing."

Neither Jonathan nor Billy Joe heard anything but some crickets, frogs on the pond, and the soft breeze in the trees. Ben and Asa were rolling their eyes this way and that in a state of near panic. In the distance they heard the roar of an alligator and the defiant cry of a bobcat.

"What does the Yunwee Chuns Dee song say?" asked Jonathan.

"They are sending a warning to be prepared for deep

sorrow and that danger is coming to this land in the form of white men who lie, cheat, and steal, whose only love is to take what is not theirs."

Jonathan was very shaken by this pronouncement. He did not know what to think. Had something happened to Amelia? He was more anxious than ever to go find her and Georgiana. He would begin to make arrangements immediately and he was glad that Billy Joe would be staying there while he was gone.

Jonathan was very upset by the old Indian's pronouncements and wondered if there was any truth to them. All he knew was that he had to hurry to Atlanta and find Amelia. During the next three days, Wy Cha Nee Chi walked around the property as if he was searching for the exact location of the burial grounds of his ancestors.

Jonathan continued making his preparations for his trip when his long time friend, Sheriff George Johnston, and two dapperly dressed gentlemen arrived in a buggy and a cloud of dust. Jonathan could tell by the serious look on the sheriff's face that this was not just a social call. After the exchange of social graces, the sheriff introduced the two men as Mr. Hazelton and Mr. Schoonover. The sheriff produced a paper claiming Mr. Hazelton and Mr. Schoonover were the "new and rightful" owners of Castlemont, having purchased the property the day before at auction for unpaid back taxes.

Jonathan was shocked speechless, but Billy Joe was quick to challenge their claim. He demanded to know the date as to when the land had been put up for auction and by whose authority. Were all avenues to find the rightful owner explored? Were the necessary papers filed? Had notices been posted in the newspapers and on all public signboards for the required sixty days?

Neither the sheriff nor the two gentlemen were prepared for this kind of challenge. Hazelton refuted with the challenge for Jonathan to produce a title to the property, counting on all records having been destroyed in the burning of the courthouse, as was Castlemont itself.

He had told Amelia to take all the important papers, paintings, jewelry, and other valuables with her to Atlanta. He had to find her to prove his ownership of the land.

Jonathan had finally recovered sufficiently enough to confront Sheriff Johnston. "George, how long have you known me?"

"Well, Jonathan, I guess over forty years. Ever since we were little kids in school together. Remember how we used to skip school and go down skinny-dippin' in the ole swimmin' hole?" the uncomfortable sheriff responded nervously.

"George, have you ever known me to live anywhere else besides Castlemont?" questioned the angry Jonathan.

"No, sir, I haven't, and your daddy and granddaddy lived here before that," offered the sheriff. "But the taxes haven't been paid for four years, Jonathan."

"George, you are my witness to the ownership of Castlemont."

Billy Joe quickly spoke up and said, "If Mr. Stevens has lived here for over forty years and was preceded by his father and grandfather, the Homestead Act and the grandfather clause would take precedence over any other papers of ownership. How can these unknown men claim to now suddenly own Castlemont? I want to see their title to the property, the bill of sale, and who initiated the transaction, since the courthouse records were all destroyed."

Both Hazelton and Schoonover produced official-looking papers as the sheriff looked on helplessly. Billy Joe then asked if they could show him the boundary markers. The men became flustered and appealed to the confused sheriff.

Sheriff Johnston cleared his throat as he reached into his pocket and produced another document. He said, "Jonathan, I feel terrible about all of this, but I have to arrest you for contempt of congress for maintaining slaves following the Emancipation Act."

Billy Joe hollered, "Hold it, Mr. Stevens!" and jumped between Jonathan's pointed gun and the three men. Holding up his hands for attention, he asked everyone to calm down. He looked directly at Hazelton and Schoonover and said, "I am Mr. Steven's personal attorney, and we will challenge this land-grab in court. Also we will bring countercharges against you on charges of misusing the law for personal gain."

This was too much for Jonathan, who grabbed up his gun and focused it directly on the three men.

Jonathan didn't understand what the quick-thinking Billy Joe had in mind, but he lowered his gun trusting that Billy Joe had a plan. Everyone seemed to breathe a sigh of relief as Billy Joe then turned his attention to the sheriff.

"Sheriff Johnston, you will find no slaves on this property. Every person here—man, woman, and child—is a 'freedman' and a wage earner, I might say. They are remaining here by their own choice. All have an equal share in the crops to be harvested. Mr. Stevens has given them jobs so as to not leave them destitute. Those who have desired to leave have already gone. You have the freedom to question all of them individually, but your arrest warrant is nothing but a carpetbagger trick to get Mr. Stevens off his property, which rightfully belongs to him. So, Sheriff, be prepared for a lawsuit for false arrest. Gentlemen, we shall see you all in court!"

Hazelton and Schoonover began to sputter their objections and insisted that they were going to stay on 'their property.' The sheriff put his papers back in his pocket and told them to get their gear and make their camp if they wanted to, but he had urgent business back in town. He then nodded to Jonathan, climbed into his buggy, and drove back down the lane toward town in a cloud of dust. Hazelton and Schoonover decided they had better pick up their gear and head toward the river bottoms to make their camp.

That night Billy Joe gathered everyone around the campfire and unfolded "his plan" as to how they would handle the carpetbaggers.

"Folks, these carpetbaggers are city people and have no ideas about Indians in this area. Therefore, we are going to give them a good lesson as to the presence of 'wild Indians' and what they sometimes do to white men in the night."

For the next three days, Billy Joe, carrying a rifle, made it a special occasion to run into Hazelton and Schoonover as they went about scouting the area. He made it a point to fill them in on all the Indian lore, much of which he made up, and pointed out several burial grounds, one of which just happened to be near their campsite. He told them tales of "strange happenings" in the area, that often at night Indians were seen in ghostly caricature wailing and moaning for their dead, and that people who had the misfortune of walking on the graves of the unmarked burial grounds had mysteriously disappeared never to be seen again. He even allowed Wy Cha Nee Chi to be seen by them at a distance. He said the reason that he carried his rifle was that Indians had been recently sighted in the area.

Several nights later there was thunder in the distance and the smell of rain in the air. The frogs and crickets suddenly ceased their nightly serenade. Schoonover said, "Do you believe all that stuff about ghosts and Indians wailing and moaning and people disappearing?"

"I don't believe in all that garbage; Barker was just funnin' us. But last night I woke up to some funny noises. Sounded like someone was bad sick or dying."

"Yeah, and the night before I kept hearing' something like a lot of people running."

Just then a limb broke as if someone had stepped on it. Both men grew quiet. The leaves of the nearby trees rustled, but neither man could feel any breeze blowing. Strange noises once again came from the direction of the Indian burial grounds. Out of the corner of his eye, Hazelton caught sight of movement in the fringes of the firelight, which was followed by a death-like scream and the running of many feet. Both men sat there petrified. For a long time, there was absolute silence, and then the frogs and crickets once again took up their songs of the night. Both men gave a sigh of relief and looked at each other, but neither spoke.

Suddenly an arrow hit their coffee pot and spilled its contents into the fire with a loud hissing, which caused both men to jump to their feet. Again there was no other sound except the distant thunder of the coming storm. They both wished they had brought some weapons with them. Once again, it was just too quiet.

Nothing further happened, so they built up their fire for the night and crawled into their bedrolls to try to get some sleep. The thunder and lightning was much closer now, and it was beginning to rain. Several night birds called to each other, and a distant alligator roared his challenge, followed by the whinny of a horse. The men were too unnerved to move. All of a sudden, an arrow carrying a bag of black powder landed in the fire and exploded into a huge ball of fire and sparks, followed immediately by the screeching of what seemed to be a thousand Indians. Both men jumped out of their bedrolls and fled out into the night in the direction of the swamps, away from the unseen Indians who were in hot pursuit.

They were battered and mauled by low-hanging tree limbs, underbrush, and roots. Twice the savages seemed to almost catch up to them. On and on they ran toward the swamp, fighting for breath, seemingly mile after mile, fighting the terror of the night. Suddenly all was quiet, and somehow they had gotten separated. Each stood alone in the waste deep water in the middle of the swamp.

At first light, Jonathan and Billy Joe searched the carpetbaggers' campsite and found the papers they were looking for. They built a fire and dumped the bedrolls and other camping gear onto it. After everything had burned, they took branches, smoothed out the campsite, and stacked a pile of brush there so it looked as if a campsite had never existed. They returned to their own campsite confident that they had seen the last of Hazelton and Schoonover. When they arrived, everyone was still laughing over the wild Indian incident and sharing their own personal version of the event.

The stories of the escapade went on for days, each time ending in fits of laughter.

Jonathan and Billy Joe joined into the fun. "You really sounded convincing, Jacob," said Billy Joe. "And you made a fine Indian Chief. And Asa, you hit the target right on the money when your arrow hit their coffee pot. I doubt that we will see them back here again." Jonathan hadn't laughed that hard in years.

In the meantime, the night seemed to drag on forever for Percy Schoonover in the middle of the swamp. He had lost sight of Oliver and was afraid to move, so he stood in the waste-deep, slimy water to await the dawn. The constant noise of frogs, toads, birds, and insects, accompanied by the roaring and grunting of alligators, kept his nerves on edge.

Several times he felt something brush against his legs, but he was too terrified to move. Once he heard what he thought was a bear growl, and several times the squall and hiss of a wildcat. A deer even swam by. He had no idea what had happened to Oliver. All he knew was that he was alone in the middle of the swamp with what he believed to be a broken arm, but he hurt all over.

The dawn began to break when Percy heard strange noises to his left that sounded like a mixture of a strangled scream and a moan. First he thought it was the Indians returning to look for him, and he began to look for a possible hiding place.

The mist began to clear, and he was finally able to see Oliver backing toward him slowly with a giant alligator in patient, tantalizing pursuit. Somehow they had to get out of the water to safety, but which way should they go? Percy spotted a giant cypress tree about fifty feet away that had numerous knees above the water. He called to Oliver to follow him there. They were greeted by a water moccasin snake who had already claimed the tree as a residence for the day. After much splashing of water and hollering, the snake swam away, and Percy was able to climb aboard and help Oliver escape the clutching jaws of the alligator, who tore away his pant leg.

Hours passed as the men huddled on their tiny perch under the constant surveillance of the ever present alligator. The deer flies and mosquitoes swarmed in a cloud around them, adding to their misery. Both men were exhausted from fear and lack of sleep, food, and water.

Oliver had sustained a nasty gash on his forehead, which attracted the various bugs and gave him a severe headache. He had also badly wrenched his knee, which was now swollen to twice its normal size. He was having dizzy spells and once nearly fell off his perch, at which the alligator became immediately active in the water.

Percy sat in a cloud of doom. To think, they had left a profitable business in New York City to come here on a whim to get rich quick.

They had comfortable homes and were socially acceptable, and both had done well selling shoes of inferior quality at a high price to the Union army during the war. Maybe that was it! God was punishing them for what they had done. Remorsefully, Percy began to whimper a prayer asking for forgiveness.

The hours dragged by, and Oliver became more delirious and tried to climb down into the water to get a drink. Percy drug him back as the alligator's jaws snapped closed on a cypress knee, barely missing Oliver's leg again.

The late afternoon shadows had begun to fall when Percy caught sight of a dilapidated old boat, with a slovenly dressed old man, coming into sight around the bend. Percy began to shout and wave his arm as Oliver sat and whimpered.

The old "swamp-rat" spotted the stranded men and the waiting alligator. He picked up his old rifle and shot the alligator.

"What you fellers doin' out here in the middle of this here swamp?" asked the old codger. "Name's Bubba, what's yourn?"

"We're lost," said Percy. "Indians drove us out here and left us to die."

"In'juns, you say. There hain't no In'juns aroun' here! Where you fellers from anyway? Hain't been no In'juns aroun' here for nigh on to fifty years."

"My partner and I came down here from New York

City to buy property, which we did at a bargain price, but when we went to take possession of it, the Indians attacked us last night and drove us out here in the swamp to die," Percy said.

"Carpetbaggers! I might have know'd it. Should have left that ole 'gator to finish the job. In'juns you say? That's mighty pee-cul-ar. I hain't never seen no In'juns about here. They all think this here swamp is haunted. Ya hain't no revenuers now, are ya? Revuenuers and carpetbaggers hain't welcome roun' here."

"Mister, we are good law abiding citizens, but we need your help in getting us safely out of this place. We will pay you. My partner here needs a doctor real bad, and I know my arm must be broken. It hurts so bad I can hardly move it. I don't know what we would have done if you hadn't come along," said Percy. By this time, Oliver was incoherent.

"Well, I 'speck ole Mr. 'Gator would of had his'self a mighty fine dinner if'n I hadn't come along. Let's see, first off I got to get ole Mr. 'Gator tied onto the boat 'fore he sinks. That thar hide of his'n will bring a real fine price."

Bubba went about the business of securing the dead alligator to the side of the boat while Percy attempted to rouse Oliver enough to climb into the boat. Bubba next tied the boat to the cypress knees, and together they lowered the semi-conscious Oliver. The movement caused Oliver to rouse enough to open his eyes and become aware he was face to face with the now dead alligator tied to the side of the boat. He let out a terrorizing scream, dove overboard, and began thrashing in the water, screaming every time he surfaced.

Bubba and Percy had difficulty getting the boat close enough to help Oliver and finally had to wait until he had totally exhausted himself before they could once again pull him aboard. They decided they had better tie his hands and feet and blindfold him so he would not jump overboard again.

Bubba headed the boat through the various channels toward his cabin, where they made camp for the night. All through the night, Oliver was delirious and had to be tied to the makeshift bed. Bubba left Percy in charge so he could go for help. Being a recluse, he didn't want anyone to know just exactly where he lived or where he kept his still. He arranged to meet a friend with a doctor at the edge of the swamp at dawn the next morning.

He returned by midnight and settled down for a long night vigil, allowing Percy to also get some much needed rest. During the night, Bubba skinned out the alligator and disposed of the carcass. He wrapped the hide in a tarp and put it in the boat.

Dawn was breaking as he and Percy loaded the incoherent Oliver into the boat for the final trip out of the swamp and to the waiting doctor.

Dr. Samuelson was amazed that either man was still alive. Percy Schoonover's arm was now badly infected, as was Oliver Hazelton's head wound. The doctor, like Bubba and his friend, was amazed at their story of having been attacked by Indians. It didn't take long for the story to spread when Bubba embellished it at the local tavern while the men were being treated. Several patrons were eager to organize a posse and go after the Indians. Of course, they didn't know where to look, but it sounded exciting. Plus, they had had just enough to drink to make them eager to go.

During the next several days, Dr. Samuelson was worried that he would have to amputate Percy's arm. Even though he was able to set the bone, the arm would always be crooked. Finally, on the fourth day, Percy's fever broke, and the doctor knew he had won the battle. However, it would require a long recovery.

Neither of the men wanted to talk about their great land purchase or the Indian attack. Both were eager to be able to go back to New York and forget about any "get rich quick" ventures in the South.

Journey into Darkness

Scattered bits and pieces of news filtered into Castlemont regarding the sacking of Atlanta and the forming of the Freedmen's Bureau, along with the rumors of congressional injustices regarding Southern landowners. Several neighboring plantation owners had been defrauded of their lands by carpetbaggers, copperheads, and scalawags.

Jonathan was torn over his need to go to Atlanta to search for Amelia and his need to stay at Castlemont to protect the plantation from further exploitation. Everywhere there was talk of the Freedman's Bureau breaking up the big plantations by giving former slaves forty acres and a mule. Feelings were a tinder-box of explosives, and everyone was holding a flint and striker to start the fires of the final destruction of the South.

Billy Joe, Toby, and Ben assured Jonathan that they and the other Free Issue Negroes were capable of taking care of the plantation while he was away. They were anxiously waiting for the coming harvest season to begin.

Ten of the better horses had been sold at a good price

to a horse trader from Virginia, and the sawmill had been ordered. These assurances helped Jonathan make his final preparations for the 160-mile trek to Atlanta. Since he was to be away for no more than two weeks, he planned to travel light.

Jonathan spent long hours in the saddle trying to get to Atlanta in record time. The closer he got, the greater his anxiety, but he was not in any way prepared for the devastation that he found. People were shamelessly begging on every street corner. Freedmen milled about in groups for encouragement, protection, and support. People slept under any shelter they could find. The streets were ribbons of ruts and debris. It appeared as though a huge tornado had swept through the city. It was noticeable that there were no dogs, cats, possums, or even rats to be found.

Block after block of the industrial and business sections of the city had been destroyed. Fredrickson's General Mercantile Store was back in business using a large tent until a new building could be erected. There were posted guards, and only those with real money in hand were allowed to enter the store. The rail yards were a mass of twisted steel snaking its way out of the city. During the invasion, church buildings had been considered sacred sanctuaries and whenever possible were left untouched. They now stood out like monumental sentinels in the graveyard where once stood beautiful homes. Peach Tree Street was a rubbled mass of blackened chimneys, crumbled brick walls, and littered, weed-infested yards. Here and there were carriage blocks with the former owner's name etched in them, letting everyone who passed by know who had once lived there.

Wagon tracks could be seen where scavengers had pilfered any usable building materials available. Some families had cleared their own foundations and had begun new construction with scraps and pieces of lumber and brick from anywhere they could find it. Everyone seemed to be moving in a daze.

James and Georgiana's house was nothing but a pile of ashes and discolored broken brick. No one seemed to know the whereabouts of Amelia and Georgiana. Mr. Brodrick, a neighbor, said he had heard that James had been killed in the battle of Ezra Church. This news hit Jonathan with a terrible blow and made him more frantic in his search to find Amelia and Georgiana.

It began to rain and continued for the next three days as Jonathan, like a man possessed, stopped everyone he saw to inquire about Amelia, but no one seemed to know. On the fourth day, he met the vicar of St. James Church, who told him the long feared news that in the initial assault of Sherman's armies, the house had taken a direct hit from artillery fire and had burned to the ground. No one had seen them since.

Something snapped in Jonathan. First he had lost Johnny Boy, then his arm, followed by the destruction of Castlemont, and now the deaths of James, Amelia, and Georgiana. All was gone—gone! His mind would not focus. Life had dealt its final blow. Jonathan aimlessly wandered down the street of oblivion, leading his horse out of the city unaware of anyone or anything.

"Hey, mister! Are you all right?"

Jonathan looked with vacant, uncomprehending eyes at Zedikiah Rogers, an itinerant preacher who was bending over him. He couldn't remember where he was, what day it was, who he was, or when he had last eaten. Nothing was in focus. His mind had deserted him, shutting down completely.

The preacher could tell that this haggard man, like so many returning soldiers, had suffered a great trauma.

"Mister, what's your name?"

Jonathan made no response.

"That's a fine horse you have there."

Jonathan roused from his stupor in a panic to protect his horse.

"Mister, I don't want your horse; I just want to help you. You seem to be in real bad shape."

Again Jonathan made no response except to huddle like a crab in a fetal position at the feet of his horse and desperately held on to the halter rope. He had a wild, demonic look on his face. His clothes were filthy and his hair and beard matted, for he had wandered for days in a trance-like stupor without having bathed, shaved, or eaten.

The preacher decided to build a fire and prepare some food. The aroma of the frying bacon, pan bread, and barley coffee caused Jonathan to glance fleetingly toward the fire. The preacher offered Jonathan a plate of food, which was snatched away and wolfed down by the famished man who once again withdrew into his inner-wounded shell like a turtle.

The preacher put more wood on the fire for the night and settled down to read aloud from his Bible. "The Lord is my shepherd, I shall not want."

"No! No! It's a lie!" screamed Jonathan. "He hates me."

He crumpled down and began to sob hysterically. Preacher Rogers was deeply troubled as to what that was all about. What was he going to do about this wounded creature of a man? He couldn't just go off and leave him by himself. He then began to pray out loud.

"Almighty God, you promised to never leave us or forsake us."

"It's a lie! It's a lie! He curses us! He destroys everything!" cried out Jonathan in his insane agony.

"No, mister, God loves us even when we go through times that seem to be like a valley of death."

"Death! That's it! He loves death! He wants everything to die! He has put a curse on everything! He wants to destroy everything! He is trying to kill me now!" shouted Jonathan as he ran off into the night.

The preacher climbed on the horse and followed Jonathan, to once again find him lying on the ground sobbing his heart out.

"Go away! You're just like him! You want to kill me too! Well, go ahead, kill me! There is nothing left for me to live for. Kill me! Please, I'd be better off. Kill me! Please kill me!"

The preacher was jolted by this outburst but began to talk softly to Jonathan as he prayed quietly for God to give him direction and insight as to how to help this terribly distraught man. At last he was able to lead Jonathan back to the fire, where he settled down for the night to sleep.

Jonathan slept the troubled sleep of a drugged man. Long after sunrise, he awoke to find the preacher reading his Bible and drinking barley coffee.

"Good morning. Are you ready for some breakfast?" asked the preacher.

"Who are you? Where did you come from? Where am I anyway?" asked Jonathan, seeming to have no recollection of their past meeting. Suspiciously Jonathan looked around until his eyes focused on his horse.

"Mister, can you remember your name this morning? And by the way, who are Johnny Boy and Amelia? You called out their names in your sleep."

"I don't know any Johnny Boy or Amelia," Jonathan said hastily, but suddenly tears began to roll uncontrollably down his cheeks. "I don't know. I don't know anything or anybody. I don't even know myself," Jonathan said in a subdued whisper.

"Well, maybe you will be able to remember after you have had some breakfast. Here, have a cup of coffee for starts." The preacher then stood up and began to stir up the fire to make griddle cakes to go with the bacon.

"I'm not hungry," said Jonathan, even though he was famished. He didn't think he deserved to eat but didn't know why he felt that way, but he did end up eating a little.

After they had eaten, the preacher said, "Well, mister, we are going to have to find out who you are and where you live. Why don't we go back into the city and ask around? Maybe we will run into someone who knows you."

"No! I don't want to go into that city. Cities are bad!" Jonathan said, but he didn't understand why he had said that.

"But you need to see a doctor."

"No! No!" Jonathan cried like a frightened child. "Doctors hurt people!" He began to tremble all over, faintly remembering sketches of the removal of his right arm.

The preacher once again realized that he had a very hurt and confused man on his hands and that it was going to take time for the man to recover. He felt God would have him stand by Jonathan until such a time as he could make it on his own.

"Mister, why don't you go through all your pockets and saddlebags to see if there are any papers that might give us a clue as to who you are?" the preacher said.

"No! No! There is nothing. There is nobody; I am nobody and from nowhere. There is nothing left," Jonathan declared in alarm. "You go away and leave me alone. I don't want your help, you…you God-devil, you! You just want to torment me. Go away."

Jonathan was suddenly very tired and decided to take a nap even though he had only been awake for about an hour.

As Jonathan slept with troubled dreams, the preacher went through Jonathan's saddlebags and coat pockets looking for clues as to the man's identity. He found a letter of introduction for the bank in Atlanta that revealed Jonathan's name and a place called Castlemont. Quietly the preacher bent over the sleeping Jonathan and began to softly call his name.

"Jonathan, Jonathan Stevens."

"Who said that? Who's calling me?" Jonathan muttered in his sleep. "Is that you, Billy Joe? Leave me alone, Billy Joe, can't you see I am trying to sleep? I don't want to talk right now. I am so tired. Billy Joe, has Johnny Boy come home yet? Have you heard from Amelia and Georgiana?" Jonathan rolled over and thrashed about in troubled sleep. "No! No! Billy Joe, they are all dead." With that Jonathan was jolted awake.

"Well, Jonathan, did you have a good rest?"

"Why did you call me Jonathan?" he asked suspiciously.

"Well, while you were asleep, I took the liberty to go through your saddlebags and coat pockets, and I found these papers that bear the name of Jonathan Stevens and a place called Castlemont."

Jonathan sat lost in deep thought, mulling over the name Castlemont.

"Castlemont. Castlemont. I've got to find Billy Joe."

"Jonathan, think hard now, can you remember where Castlemont is located?"

"Castlemont," mumbled the confused Jonathan. "East of Atlanta, a long ways," he blurted out as snatches of memory began to return.

"Jonathan, let's go back to Atlanta and inquire around. Maybe you will be able to remember more of your background. We maybe can find someone who actually knows you."

"I don't want to go to Atlanta! Atlanta is a bad place! Real bad! People get hurt and die in Atlanta."

Again Jonathan couldn't explain why he had said that, but there was a certain foreboding that hung like a storm cloud of doom over his confused mind. Together they headed toward Atlanta, Jonathan riding the horse, the preacher walking beside them.

The closer they came to the city, the more agitated Jonathan became. When they neared Peach Tree Street and the sight where James and Georgiana's burned home had stood, Jonathan's eyes were filled with tears, and his head sagged. The preacher noted the change and stopped the horse.

"Jonathan, is this where Castlemont was?"

"No!" shouted Jonathan as he cast a bewildered look over the desolate place. His mind still refused to function. They continued their way on down to the general store, where the preacher bought some supplies and asked a few questions. As they were leaving, the vicar of St. James walked up and spoke to Jonathan, who stared back with vacant eyes.

The preacher spoke up and said, "Sir, do you know this man?"

"Why, yes, I believe this is Jonathan Stevens. He and his lovely wife, Amelia, and their daughter and son-in-law used to attend services at St. James."

"Where is his family now?" the preacher asked.

The vicar's countenance dropped as he looked at the ground, unable to look at Jonathan.

"They are believed to be dead, sir, killed in the major attack upon the city."

Jonathan let out a deep agonizing moan, fainting as he fell off the horse. Quickly a crowd gathered around, and someone went for the doctor. The preacher and vicar knelt and began to pray as a hush fell over the crowd.

Dr. McCormick soon arrived and began to check Jonathan's vital signs and for any broken bones. He then administered smelling salts, which aroused Jonathan. The doctor ordered Jonathan to be taken to one of the many temporary hospitals, one of which was in the nearby Baptist church. Jonathan had withdrawn into a darkened cave of obscurity and would respond to no one. The doctor administered some laudanum, ordered complete bed rest for Jonathan, and said that he would need to be watched day and night.

The itinerant preacher, doctor, and the vicar put their heads together to try to figure out what they could do to help Jonathan.

"He kept babbling about someone called Billy Joe. Could that be one of his sons?" the preacher asked again.

"To my knowledge, there were only the two children, a son named Johnny Boy, who I believe was killed in the war, and the daughter, Georgiana," remarked the vicar.

"He needs to have someone who knows him. Do either of you know where he lived?" asked the doctor.

"He has papers referring to a place called Castlemont, and he mentioned that it was east of Atlanta, a long way east. The name sounds like it may be a plantation," reported Preacher Rogers.

"Maybe we had better see if we can find someone who knows the whereabouts of Castlemont and see if this Billy Joe is there. He could be one of the former slaves, or the overseer, or even a relative of some kind," said the doctor.

Within a few hours, one of Jonathan's former slaves came up having overheard the questions being asked. "I knows Mastuh Stevens; I's from Castlemont. I's was one of his slaves." He then agreed to make the long trip back to Castlemont if someone could provide him with a horse or a mule to ride. In the meantime, Jonathan lay in a drug-induced sleep, often crying out in terror as nightmare followed nightmare.

Two weeks later, Billy Joe, Toby, and Mammy Lou walked into the hospital. They had driven their wagon long hours each day from Castlemont, only stopping long enough to rest and feed the horses. Billy Joe sat down beside Jonathan's bed and began to talk softly to him as Mammy Lou brushed the hair back from his forehead, crooning soft words to him as if he were a small child. The doctor had warned them of Jonathan's condition, but they were shocked to see the emaciated body of the distraught man. Jonathan had not taken notice of their entrance. He just lay there staring into space like a breathing dead man.

"Mr. Stevens, it's me, Billy Joe. I came as quickly as I got word, and I brought Toby and Mammy Lou. Mr. Stevens, everything is just fine back home. Ben and Asa are looking after things. The sawmill has arrived and is being put together. It should be ready to use in another couple of weeks. The men and women have started picking cotton. There is also a real good crop of tobacco."

Jonathan never blinked an eye or changed position. He was lost in a world of utter despair. After sitting by the bedside for another fifteen minutes, Billy Joe got up, and they left the room as two tears flowed down Jonathan's cheeks.

Every day one of them and the preacher would sit beside Jonathan's bed. Billy Joe would talk about Castlemont, and the preacher would silently pray. Toby talked about the good times of the past, and Mammy Lou would sing softly to her deeply wounded child-patient. They had developed a close kinship because of their love for the Lord and concern for Jonathan. Their main objective now was Jonathan's recovery.

As the days passed, Jonathan slowly began to respond with questions or outbursts of anger. He refused to let them talk about God, pray out loud, or read from the Bible. From what they could gather, Jonathan believed God had cursed him and was punishing him for his sins. Often he was found with tears flowing shamelessly down his cheeks.

After three more weeks of convalescence, the doctor finally consented to allow them to take Jonathan back home to Castlemont. It was now mid October, and the days were still warm and the nights balmy. They loaded Jonathan carefully into the back of the wagon on a bed of fresh straw with Toby and Mammy Lou beside him. Billy Joe and the preacher sat on the wagon seat and drove the horses. Every day along the way, Jonathan became a little more responsive to what was going on around him. He even pointed at several landmarks.

They traveled slowly, averaging about ten to fifteen miles a day. At night they camped beside a river or in the yard of a farm or plantation. Jonathan's interest in life began to perk up more and more as familiar landmarks came into view. He would occasionally mutter the name of a special landmark, town, or plantation. Most of the time, Jonathan stayed within the cocoon of his oblivion. The closer they got to Castlemont, the more often his tears would flow.

It was dark when they finally arrived home. Jonathan was asleep in the wagon, so they decided not to disturb him. The horses were unhitched, watered, and fed. Billy Joe and the preacher once again slept beside the wagon to be near Jonathan. Toby and Mammy Lou went to their own little shelter for the night.

Each day Jonathan continued to improve and take a greater interest in life about him. He took comfort that the old dog, Major, never left his side. The harvest was over, Wy Cha Nee Chi had died while Jonathan had made his trip to Atlanta, and Ben had seen that he was buried according to his wishes in his ancestral burial ground. The new sawmill was running smoothly with growing stacks of drying lumber. People from miles around came daily to buy lumber with their limited harvest money and promises to pay from harvests to come. Billy Joe became the business manager and handled all the transactions. One of the first things the harvest monies were used for was to allow everyone to buy a new set of clothing and shoes for themselves. This was an exciting time for most of the Negro families at Castlemont because they had never had store-bought clothes.

The preacher held worship services under the giant oak trees until the new church building could be built. Some neighbors criticized Jonathan "for allowin' darkies to sit in church with white folks." Nevertheless, most felt a need for God, and there was always a big crowd at the worship services of both black and white folks, along with those who had been wealthy and those who were poor.

The services were followed by a dinner prepared by everyone who had food to share. Everyone was allowed to eat together at the same time, again causing dismay among some of the white folks and hesitancy among some of the Negroes, especially among those from the surrounding plantations.

The preacher and Billy Joe took turns doing the preaching. Their sermons were always practical lessons from the Bible about God's love and grace, how it should be applied to all their lives, and how they must learn to love one another and help one another to reach their own greatest potential.

Jonathan was functioning much better and began to accept the plan of "shared responsibility" as presented in Billy Joe's "story." He finally agreed to allow the plantation to be divided equally among the twelve chosen leaders, or tenant farmers, and he was to remain as the landowner and overseer. They were chosen in the style of the twelve apostles of Christ as found in the New Testament. Every one of the former slaves who had stayed were designated a job or a trade according to his or her interest and talented ability.

Jonathan, Billy Joe, and Ben were appointed to be the overseers to handle business interests for everyone. Jonathan was the owner, and Billy Joe was president since he was a lawyer. Ben was given the responsibility to be the overall foreman and spokesperson for the Negroes, seeing to their personal needs. Toby, by personal choice, was to remain as Jonathan's personal servant and assistant. All of the land stewards were appointed as an advisory or consultant council to Jonathan and Billy Joe.

Together they planned the building sites and worked out the schedule for when they were to be built. A plot of land was set aside on the main road near the entrance to Castlemont for the church, a school, and houses for the schoolteacher and the preacher. Mr. Hayes had been hired to supervise the logging and sawmill operations. He and his family were from Kentucky, and they were also Christians. He built himself a little shack for his family beside the mill so he would be close by at all times.

Jonathan had many questions about this new life venture. He had to fight the trauma of the past, with its traditions and the deaths within his family. He knew the only family he really had now were those who had befriended him and were now living on the plantation.

He was made aware that this "new plan" did not sit well with his neighbors. As the news spread, his neighbors began to drop by "to be sociable" and offer their "sound advice." All felt Jonathan was "a little tetched" to try such a foolhardy thing.

The more Jonathan recovered, the more exhilarating the plan became to him. Jonathan, at times, still had trouble with giving God credit, but he went along with Billy Joe and the preacher because he knew he could not get along without them. It soon became noticeable that Castlemont was recovering faster than the plantations of their jealous neighbors. More than once, Jonathan and Billy Joe had been jeered as "Yankee abolitionists" when they had gone to town for supplies.

Billy Joe worked out lease agreements for the appointed twelve land stewards who were to be in charge of farming the land. He also developed a wage agreement for each of the tradesmen. The carpenters would work for a portion of the harvest wages for those for whom they worked, as would the masons, blacksmiths, laborers, and servants. Everyone would pay a tithe of their income to the church, and the preacher and the council would disperse those monies for those interests that involved the church.

It was decided that the first buildings to be built would be the tobacco-drying sheds because the tobacco harvest was upon them. Next, homes would be built for Toby and Mammy Lou and the widows, followed by homes for the tradesmen, servants, and laborers. The last houses to be built were for the twelve land stewards, to be followed by a modest house for Jonathan and Billy Joe. Next would be the church building and the school. Then the barns, smokehouse, and chicken houses were to be built.

There was so much to do, and everyone worked hard from dawn till dark. However, everyone rested and attended the worship services on the Lord's Day. Benji, Ben's grandson, appointed himself to be Jonathan's inseparable companion and was somewhat jealous of Toby's presence. He was only six years old now, but he was able to sense Jonathan's need for love and understanding. They would occasionally be seen heading for the river to fish or swim with the old collie dog tagging along behind.

One day as Benji and Jonathan sat under a tree fishing, Benji asked Jonathan, "Mastuh Jon Jon, wher's your momma? Poppa say you had a big boy like me, but he dead."

Jonathan was taken aback by these forthright questions from young Benji and carefully thought how he might answer.

"I used to have a beautiful wife named Amelia, a son, Johnny Boy, named after me, and a daughter named Georgiana, but they aren't here anymore."

Jonathan had never discussed their deaths with anyone; in fact, he would not allow himself to think of them as dead. The pain and loneliness was too overwheming.

"Mastuh Jon Jon, is da dead?"

"Yes," Jonathan hesitantly whispered with tears filling his eyes. It now seemed so final.

"Did they go to hea'ben like Poppa say?" asked the innocent child.

"I hope so."

"Are you go'in to hea'ben when you dies, Mastuh Jon Jon? The preacher, he say if you love God and believe in his Son as da Lawd, yo'll go to hea'ben. Do youse believe that, Mastuh Jon Jon?"

"I hope so, I really hope so,"

"Don't you know, Mastuh Jon Jon?"

"I'm not sure. I'm just not sure about anything right now."

"My poppa, he say God loves ever'body, and he don't want nobody to die and not go to hea'ben. My poppa, he say he's go'in to hea'ben for shore," the young Benji said proudly.

"Your poppa is a good man, and your momma a good

woman." Jonathan tried to think of a way to distract the child's attention to talk about something else.

"How did your momma die, Mastuh Jon Jon?"

"I don't know; no one seems to know. That's the hard part; no one seems to know." And with that the tears began to roll down Jonathan's cheeks.

"Mastuh Jon Jon, is youse cry'in?"

"Yes, I guess I am." He then began to sob out his heart, and Benji crawled into his lap and hugged him while the old dog quietly nuzzled his knee.

Jonathan held the young child tenderly yet desperately, as if he were afraid he too might be taken away. For some time the two clung to each other in quiet understanding.

Finally, the spell was broken when Benji's forgotten fishing pole began to jerk violently and both made a grab for it. Later they were to be seen proudly walking back to camp carrying their monstrous catch of the day, a ten pound catfish.

Amelia woke from a very troubled sleep. She had dreamed about Castlemont and Jonathan sitting under a tree crying, which was not like Jonathan at all.

It had been a year since the war had ended, and no word had come concerning him. There had been a military funeral for James. His parents had received word about it four months after it had taken place. There had been no word concerning Jonathan, but of course few people knew where she was.

The railroads were back in service, and the whole

South was gradually recovering. Mr. Stewart was back working at the bank and bringing home a very meager income. Jacob and Mollie had gotten married and lived in a little house at the edge of town. He had gotten a job on the section-gang for the railroad, and their first child would be born within three months.

They were eating breakfast when Amelia told Georgiana of her dream and how distressed it had left her.

"Mother, maybe Daddy is alive and back at Castlemont," said Georgiana. "He could be, you know. Why don't you write a letter? Someone there will know."

"I don't know what to do; one minute I feel I need to rush back there right away, but part of me is afraid of what I might really find. Besides, we don't have any money for the train tickets."

"Let's talk it over with Father Stewart tonight. He will know what to do."

The day seemed to drag on forever for Amelia. Each hour seemed to be a year in coming as the tension grew and grew.

During the evening dinner, Mr. Stewart said, "Amelia, you don't seem to be yourself this evening. Is something wrong?"

Georgiana answered her father-in-law as Amelia burst into tears. "Father Stewart, Mother had this dream last night about Daddy and she doesn't know what to do. She thinks that he might still be alive and back at Castlemont and that she should go, but she's afraid to. And besides, we don't have the money for her to go."

Mother Stewart spoke up. "My dear girl, there are

some things that cannot wait. We'll just have to pool our resources and get the money. This is just too important. Amelia, you do want to go desperately, don't you, dear?"

All Amelia could do was nod her head between sobs.

"Then Mr. Stewart and I will help, won't we, dear?" assured Mrs. Stewart.

"By all means, my dear. I will check the train schedules and the price of the tickets first thing in the morning. Georgiana, I think you should go with your mother. Mrs. Winslow at the dress shop will understand and hold your job if necessary."

Both Amelia and Georgiana were overcome with tears at this announcement and sobbed in each other's arms, dinner long forgotten.

They talked far into the night, making plans for their trip of unknown destiny. All they had left of value to sell were their wedding rings. Both felt it was necessary to sacrifice them, but that meant letting go of something too sacred to talk about.

"What are we going to do if Daddy is not there? I even wonder if we still own Castlemont or if there is even anyone there. It is scary just to think about it," said Georgiana.

"I don't know what to think. One minute I want to be there, and the next I am scared to death of what we will find. I don't know anything about running a plantation. Jonathan and Mr. Alexander always took care of those things. I know when Mr. Alexander left for the war, I felt so helpless, and so I turned everything over to Ben and Toby. That was all I could do."

"What will we do if no one is there and we discover that we no longer own Castlemont?"

"Well, we won't know until we get there, that is for sure."

The next day, after considerable discussion, Mr. Stewart took the rings to find a buyer. He felt there just had to be some other way to purchase the tickets without severing all ties with the past, but by now the feeling to go was most urgent.

Mr. Stewart sold the rings through personal connections for considerably more than the cost of the tickets. This would help meet their other financial needs as well those that would come up along the way. By now the two women were in a near frenzy in preparing for their trip.

Their first Christmas back at Castlemont was quietly observed with a special worship service, and everyone gathered to sing the Christmas carols, which was followed by a dinner. The children each received a small gift and an orange.

Over the months house after house had taken shape with a small celebration or housewarming party upon its completion. There was singing and dancing and of course special little token gifts for the new home.

It was now time to plant the spring crops, so those who were not directly involved with the building of houses gave their attention to putting in the crops. It was exciting to see some of the neglected fields once again spring to life, having had the brush cleared and being plowed up, ready to receive the new crop. The new land stewards, or tenant farmers, worked hard with everyone pitching in to make it a great harvest because everyone would have a share in the proceeds of the crop. Yes, it was truly a new beginning for Castlemont.

There was a lull after the spring planting and the coming harvest, so it was time to build the church. It had been a year now since Jonathan first returned to the ashes of Castlemont, and he was so proud to see all the beautiful things that were taking place. He just wished that Amelia was there to enjoy it with him.

After much planning, they were ready to build the church. Jonathan and Billy Joe figured that with all the help they had, the church could be completed within a week. The ladies would provide the food for each day, and Jonathan would provide the meat for each day's barbeque.

Jonathan carefully laid out the construction plans with Billy Joe and instructed everyone on just how they would raise the building. They would work as teams, each doing special jobs. Part of the crew would work on putting together the rafters while others laid the foundation and floors. One group would frame up the walls, and still another group would build the church pews. Yet another group would build the steeple for the bell that had always been used to call the people in from the fields. In three days the foundation, floor, and walls were up, and everyone was excited because they seemed to be ahead of schedule.

It was amazing to them to see the building grow, and

it was just natural that they began to sing their beloved songs as they worked. Sightseers and passerby even stopped to help. Jonathan and Billy Joe often took time to check the plans and compare notes.

It was amazing, and everyone was in a festive mood. Jonathan and Billy Joe stood back in the shade of a tree resting a bit while talking over the renewal of Castlemont.

"You know, Jonathan, God has been good to us and to Castlemont. He promised to pour out his blessing upon those who were faithful to him, and he certainly has, hasn't he?"

"Yes, he has, Billy Joe, I must admit. I just wish Amelia could be here to see it."

Just then someone on the roof hollered down, "Someone's comin," and all eyes focused on the road to see a horse and buggy followed by a small trail of dust. As it drew closer, they could see a driver and two ladies in the buggy.

"I wonder who that could be; I don't recognize that horse or the buggy," said Jonathan.

The horse and buggy turned into the churchyard, and a hush suddenly fell upon the crowd of workers, as all eyes were centered upon the occupants in the buggy. Amelia and Jonathan were frozen in place in total disbelief.

After a short interval, Georgiana screamed, "Daddy!" sprang out of the buggy, and ran to throw her arms around her father. Suddenly there was a frenzy of shouting that caused the dogs to bark and the horses to shy and prance about. As if in slow motion, Jonathan and Amelia ran into each other's arms and desperately clung to each other, unable to say a word. Mammy Lou had soon found Georgiana, and they were clinging to each other, crying hysterically as they danced up and down, while others gathered around.

"Praise de Lawd! Praise de Lawd!" shouted all the people as they excitedly jumped up and down with tears of joy as they gathered around Jonathan and Amelia. "The Lawd, he done brought back our Missus Stevens! Praise de Lawd!"

Finally, Georgiana disentangled herself from the arms of her parents and turned, facing Billy Joe, who stepped forward and introduced himself. "You must be the Georgiana Stewart that I have heard so much about. My name is Billy Joe Barker. I live here and help Mr. Stevens run the plantation."

Georgiana took his extended hand and said, "Yes, I am Georgiana, but, Mr. Barker, what happened to my father? He is missing an arm."

"It's a long story, Mrs. Stewart. Let's walk over to the trees out of this hot sun, and I will try to bring you up to date. Your father has been through a lot. He is not the same man you remembered him to be. War is a terrible thing. It not only destroys men's homes, it is so traumatic that it destroys their very inner-being, their soul, you might say. It destroys their dreams, their egos, and sometimes their will to even live. That was what has happened to your father. He is recovering from a complete emotional breakdown. Losing his arm, Johnny Boy, and the slaves, as well as the destruction of Castlemont, was devastating. The loss of your mother and you was the final blow."

Georgiana quietly responded. "I see. But we are here now. That will make a difference, won't it?"

"Yes," said Billy Joe, "that will make a big difference, but don't expect an overnight miracle. Your father might even go back into a period of withdrawals because his mind is very fragile at this point and cannot tolerate too many sudden changes. It will be important that you and your mother do not try to push him in decision making in any way until he gets used to you again. After all, to him, you have just risen from the dead."

"That's a strange feeling, Mr. Barker," the subdued Georgiana replied.

"Miss Georgiana, I mean, Mrs. Stewart, we'll probably be seeing quite a lot of each other in the future, so I would feel more comfortable it you would just call me Billy Joe as everyone else does."

"Then, Billy Joe, I would like it if you would call me Georgiana. I am not really Mrs. Stewart anymore since James was killed in the terrible war." Her eyes began to mist over. "I'm just Georgiana!"

Billy Joe cleared his throat and kicked his toe in the dust.

"Georgiana, I'm terribly sorry about your husband. Every one of us were losers in the war."

Jonathan and Amelia continued to cling to each other and weep, both so overcome with emotion that neither could find words to express their deep feelings of need, anguish, and hurt. There was so much to say and talk about, but neither could find words to begin. At the present, they were willing to let their hugs do the talking for them.

Jonathan finally became aware of someone pulling on his pant leg and looked down to see Benji looking up with big questioning eyes.

"Mastuh Jon Jon, is dis your momma?"

Jonathan reached down with his one arm and picked him up.

"Benji, I want you to meet my wife. Amelia, this is my special little friend, Benji."

"But Mastuh Jon Jon, youse told me dat she was dead and gone to hea'ben! How can she be here if she be dead?" asked the puzzled Benji.

"Well, I was mistaken. We just thought she was dead. But she is alive and she has come home." Jonathan said as he looked at Amelia with misty eyes.

"Benji, my, how you have grown into a big boy since I last saw you before I left Castlemont. You were just a little boy then."

Asa quickly came over, took Benji from Jonathan, and turned to the crowd of happy workers.

Ben called, "Hey thar, youse lazy niggers, we'uns gots us a chu'ch house ta finish buildin' t'day."

The magic spell was broken, and everyone left Jonathan and Amelia to themselves and returned more joyous than ever to their labor. Tomorrow would really be a day of worship and praise, and it would be in their new church building with a tall spiraling steeple with a bell in it. Jonathan and Amelia looked at each other from head to toe as if they were trying to comprehend the reality of finding each other. It was then that Amelia noticed that Jonathan was missing his right arm. She burst into tears all over again as she cried out, "Jonathan, you have been hurt! What happened? Oh, you poor, dear man!"

She once again threw her arms around Jonathan. He was too overcome to even reply. Quietly they withdrew to the shade of the trees where they could sit down and begin to put their shattered lives back together again. Jonathan was hesitant to talk much about the war. He was finally able to tell her about being wounded but would not discuss the removal of his arm. The memory was just too painful. They talked a little about Johnny Boy and James and cried some more. Someone brought them a cold drink of water.

It was a time of sorrow, yet a time of rejoicing and rebirth. There was so much to look forward to and so many adjustments to be made. It was a time of leaving the past behind and looking forward to new beginnings, although Jonathan was still in a state of shock. "How long have you been back, Jonathan, and who is that young man talking to Georgiana?"

"I got back in May, and the young man is Billy Joe Barker, a young Yankee soldier who was raised here in the South. He has been a lot of help to me in getting things lined out to rebuild Castlemont."

"A Yankee soldier! What have you got a Yankee soldier here for?"

"Well, I really needed someone to help me get organized, and I had no overseer to rely on. And he is very capable. He is a lawyer and saved Castlemont for me from carpetbaggers."

Amelia told him some about her stay with Georgiana in Atlanta, their harrowing escape from the city under siege, and the long difficult time it took them to get James' parents in Birmingham. "Jacob, Molly, and Sarah were with us, and they are now staying with the Stewarts." They both talked about their fears that the other had been lost.

The late afternoon shadows were falling when finally the steeple was placed and someone tried ringing the bell as a test run. The painters were working feverishly to complete their part of the job before it was too dark to see. Billy Joe and Preacher Rogers began making preparations for the next day's services to be followed by a dinner under the trees. The new pews had even been placed inside the church.

There had even been messengers sent throughout the area announcing the arrival of Amelia and Georgiana and that there would be services "in the new church" the next day. After all the work was done, a bonfire was built from the remaining scraps of lumber, and the people, though exhausted, gathered around for a spontaneous time of praise. Jonathan and Amelia stayed in the shadows and listened.

This was something new and challenging for Amelia. It was intriguing, yet foreign to her upbringing, for it was not traditional. This was what the Negroes did, and she had never been a part of anything like it, for it had not been proper. She was kind of in awe. Jonathan held her hand and bowed his head as the tears flowed. In spite of it all, it was wonderful to be alive.

The fire burned itself down to just a bed of embers as mothers gathered up their sleeping children, and families quietly slipped off into the night to their new homes.

Ben and his wife, Beulah, told Jonathan and Amelia that they had prepared their home for them to stay in until their own house could be built. Both Jonathan and Amelia started to protest that they would be causing a great inconvenience for Ben and his family, but Ben and Beulah would have it no other way. The preparations had already been made.

Benji sleepily said, "Mastuh Jon Jon, youse staying at my grandpa's house."

Amelia was incensed; who were these "slaves" to tell Jonathan where they were going to stay? She was having serious misgivings about sleeping in a "darkie's" bed. What would her friends think? She would die of mortification if they were to ever find out. Social standing and priorities were deeply engrained in Amelia. In her mind, one just did not under any circumstance put oneself in a questionable situation.

If it hadn't been so late and if she hadn't been so tired, she would have absolutely insisted that Jonathan drive her into Cedar Crossing so they could stay in the hotel like decent white folks should. She even thought about making do in a makeshift tent of some kind. Her staying in a darkie's house was unheard of. They reached Ben and Beulah's house and discovered that indeed Ben's family's personal things had already been removed and their own had been laid out awaiting their arrival. Jonathan left Amelia so he could escort Georgiana to Mammy Lou and Toby's house but was soon intercepted by Billy Joe, who offered to show Georgiana the way. Jonathan returned to the house to find that Amelia had quickly changed into her nightclothes and was sitting on the side of the bed brushing her beautiful raven-black hair. For a long moment, he quietly stood watching her until she stood and raised her arms to welcome him to her embrace. He took her in his arm as he gently pulled her to the bed, and soon, for that night, all their painful memories were forgotten.

The Great Day of Praise

The morning dawn found Billy Joe and the preacher kneeling at the new church altar in prayer. They felt the whole future of Castlemont and the surrounding community depended upon the success of this first day of worship. They knew that there was still a lot of hostility, prejudice, and anger in the hearts of many of the area people. They prayed that the Holy Ghost would prepare and soften the hearts of the people so social and spiritual changes could take place.

They prayed that they would be able to speak what they believed the Holy Ghost would want the people to hear. They continued to pray that God would bring only those who would be eager to hear what God would have them hear, but above all they prayed for God's loving grace to flow over everyone.

They also prayed that they, as God's witnesses, might be used as holy vessels to pour forth God's special anointing upon his people. It was a challenging opportunity, and they did not want to fail the Lord.

The worship service had been set to start at ten thirty

that Sunday morning, but people began to arrive an hour and a half early. Many said that they wanted to be there early so that they could see the others arrive, so they sat or stood under the trees to watch the arriving crowd. Someone had started a fire and put on a big pot of coffee for the gathering crowd.

Everyone was excited and amazed as people came from all directions. They arrived in wagons, carts, buggies, and on horseback or mule, and many walked. Some had started hours earlier to arrive on time for the services. It was amazing how far the news had traveled in such a short time. There were so many people that they could not begin to get everyone into the new church building, so Billy Joe and the preacher decided to begin the service outside to accommodate the overflowing crowd, using the new porch as the chancel and podium.

The church pews had been moved outside for the ladies and older people to sit on during the service. The others would either stand or sit on blankets on the ground.

Everyone had been encouraged to bring what musical instruments they had to form an orchestra of sorts. There was an assortment of banjos, fiddles, and mouth harps, as well as an accordion or two and a trumpet.

The musicians tuned their instruments the best they could, and the service began with Billy Joe asking everyone to stand and bow their heads as Preacher Rogers led them in the opening prayer. This was followed by a mix of the great hymns of the church and Negro spirituals. There was time given for those who wanted to stand and express their personal thanksgiving and praise, which became spontaneous with many participating. Jonathan also stood and tried to express his feelings but became so choked up he could only bow his head and let his tears speak for him.

A number of people gathered around both Jonathan and Amelia and gave them hugs. It was a precious, heart-rending time. Someone began to softly sing "Amazing Grace," and everyone else joined in. At this point the service took on a more spiritual depth, with people spontaneously singing this hymn or that spiritual, and the people clapped and swayed with the mood of the song. Time was forgotten, and all felt that God was in their presence.

After some time Preacher Rogers stood and began to speak from the Old Testament, about how God had instructed Solomon, whose name meant "man of peace," to use his great wisdom to build the temple. God instructed Solomon to use the best craftsmen and best of materials that could be found. The temple was to be built to draw all men's attention and worship to the glory of God alone, for the temple was to be God's dwelling place among his people. God's presence would be so strong in the temple that anyone entering it unclean or who tried to defile the temple in any way would be struck dead. It was at the temple that man could have his sins rolled back by presenting the right animal sacrifice. The temple was not only to be the permanent Holy Place of God, but it would also have the Holy of Holies.

The preacher also talked about the Ark of the Covenant. God had given to his people the Ark of the Covenant many years before as a symbol of his presence among them as he led them out of Egyptian captivity.

The ark was then placed in the Holy of Holies in the temple to symbolize God's entering and continued presence, his sustaining power, and their freedom under God's care. The candelabra and the Table of Shewbread were put into the temple to remind the people that God said, "Let there be light and there was light" (Gen. 1:3). The light was to remind the people that everything God created came from the essence of light and gave life.

All life came from God. The Table of Shewbread was to remind the people that God had and would always provide for nourishment of the physical and spiritual needs of his faithful people. He then talked about how when the temple was finished, Solomon had said, "I was glad when they said, 'Let us go up into the house of our God'" (Ps. 122:1).

"Their relationship with God was the most important thing in their lives, as it should be ours today," said Preacher Rogers.

Billy Joe then stood and picked up the story of how man had continued to be unfaithful to God. He talked about how God grieved because he had no way to save his people from their sins. God had promised to never again use a flood to destroy the sinfulness of man. Therefore, God in his great wisdom decided to come and live, in person, with his people. That way they could see and understand the true meaning of relationships for their lives. He was then born as any normal baby and dwelt among his people so they would accept him as one of them. They called him Immanuel, which meant "God is with us." His other name was Jesus, which meant "He shall save his people from their sins." God then sent his

Holy Ghost to indwell those who repented of their sin. They became holy vessels, or God's dwelling place, and there was no further need for the temple in Jerusalem, which the Romans later destroyed.

Billy Joe continued by saying, "We have built this church building not as a temple but as a place of meeting for the worship of God. Jesus died on the cross to take away our sin, not just to roll our sins back for later judgment. We who believe in Jesus as our personal Savior and Lord, our bodies become the new temple of God and the dwelling place of his Holy Ghost. Therefore, we become a holy vessel and are to pour out God's Spirit upon other people by the way we live and treat others. Our lives are not our own, for we have been purchased by the great sacrifice of God's humility and grace on the cross. Therefore, 'we are to humble ourselves before the Lord, Our God, for He alone is worthy to be praised.' We are not here to dedicate a building, but to dedicate our personal lives to God, so God, through our lives, can change the world where we live. In Christ, 'we are new creatures,' no longer to follow after our own desires and lusts of the flesh, but to live only for God's glorification. Therefore, 'all bigotry, greed, slander, untruthfulness, idolatry, and fornication, are an embarrassment to God, and destroy our relationship with Him' (Gal. 5:19–21)."

There was a real conviction as the Holy Ghost searched each heart, and the people spontaneously began to cry out begging God for forgiveness. Some were totally overcome and swooned where they sat or stood. There was not a dry eye or an unconvicted heart to be found. It was truly a new beginning. But as with all new beginnings, adversity would soon follow.

The next day there was a subdued mood among the people of Castlemont. It was as if they did not want to end the services of yesterday. They had reached a mountaintop and did not want to return to the valleys or the struggles of the climb. Jonathan and Billy Joe called the council members together, and they all decided that since everyone had been working so hard for so long, they all needed a week to rest before the start of the fall harvest.

This was most unusual, and at first the former slaves stood silently in disbelief because it had never happened before. Billy Joe reminded them that this was part of the new way since they were Free Issue and no longer slaves. They were free to sleep late, free to go fishing, and free to visit among themselves or relatives on other plantations. They could work for themselves around their own places or go to the nearby town of Cedar Crossing to shop. Whatever they chose to do, they were free to do it.

For a long time they just stood huddled in small groups trying to digest their newfound freedom and decide what they really wanted to do most. Gradually several found their fishing poles and headed for the river while others started to work in their gardens.

Amelia and Georgiana were amazed, momentarily forgetting that the former slaves were now freedmen. What was happening to Castlemont? Had Jonathan truly lost his mind and given Castlemont away? Slaves had never been given a week off from their labors. Why, they might start a rebellion, or they could run away! This had to be stopped. There would soon be no one left to do the work.

Amelia could not understand why the mansion had not been the first of the buildings to be rebuilt. After all, Jonathan was the owner and master of Castlemont. She would have to speak to Jonathan immediately.

Early that afternoon she arranged for Jonathan and her to take a walk down by the river at their favorite spot. There she demanded some answers. She brought up the subject by saying, "Jonathan, I need to know what is going on here. It appears that you are no longer yourself and certainly not the man I married. You have changed. You have let this abolitionist, Billy Joe, take control of Castlemont. He is making a fool out of you and the whole South with all these newfangled abolitionist ideas. Jonathan, this is the South! We have our traditions and proprieties! You have made us the laughingstock of the whole South! I won't stand for it. How could you do this to me?"

Jonathan's calm response was, "Amelia, times are changing, and we have to be willing to change with them. The South will never again be as it used to be."

Amelia was incensed. "If you expect me to accept all that poppy-cock of change and religion, you've got another think a'coming. And another thing, I will not stay another night in that darkie's house. I am so embarrassed I could die. Georgiana and I will be leaving immediately and going to Savannah to stay with Aunt

Birdie until you come to your senses, rebuild the mansion as it was, and start running Castlemont as it used to be. And another thing, that abolitionist preacher with all his new fancy ideas has got to go. White folks sitting side-by-side with black folks and eating at the same table with them is outrageous. We have our proprieties. They are supposed to keep their place. They are just like the poor cracker white trash that were there. That church service was nothing like what we are used to in Atlanta. It was too emotional, and this has got to stop!"

Needless to say, Amelia was still in a state of shock at Jonathan's handicap and the fact that he had not built her a home that was like what she was used to having before the war. She wanted to have the mansion rebuilt now, and she was used to having her own way. She had hoped that all the hardships of the war would be over and was very disappointed.

After that statement Amelia marched back to start packing and left Jonathan with his head hanging in remorse. What was he going to do? Was he going to lose Amelia after finally finding her? She was the very center of his life. How was he going to turn back the pages of time to please her?

Jonathan began to think his worst thoughts. *She doesn't love me anymore. I lost my arm, and she thinks I am not man enough to run Castlemont!* He was truly caught in a depressing dilemma.

He slowly began to walk along the riverbank trying to think out the whole situation. So much had happened that he didn't know where to start. He thought about his early childhood at Castlemont, the fun he had riding his pony with his father and brother, the times they had gone fishing and swimming together, in this same river. He could almost hear their laughter and shouts of joy.

Christmas was always very special with all their cousins and other relatives coming for a whole week, the excitement of searching the house and barns for hidden gifts that were too big to put under the tree. He remembered he was five years old the Christmas he had gotten his first pony. He remembered how he had dreamed of owning his own pony, and there it was, a beautiful little bay with a black mane. His brother's pony was black. All their other gifts were quickly forgotten that year, and they nearly had to be dragged off the ponies when dinner was served. That night both the ponies and little boys were exhausted.

Castlemont was well known for its festive parties, such as the annual harvest barbecue, Christmas with all the relatives, and the New Year's parties for all their friends for miles around. Not to be overlooked were the summer picnics and dinner parties.

There were always so many children with games of Blind Man's Bluff, Hide and Seek, Run Rover Run, Kick the Can, baseball, and other games. Of course in the summer time, all the boys got to go swimming, much to the envy of the girls who had to stay behind, the little ones to play with their dolls. The older, more sophisticated girls strolled through the gardens and had been known to sneak down to the river and peek through the bushes where the boys were swimming, sometimes in the raw.

There was a giant oak tree that stood out over the swimming hole, and Jonathan's father had had one of the slaves hang a big rope from one of the stout limbs. What fun they had swinging out over the water and letting go, everyone trying to out-do the others as to who could make the biggest splash. Life was so carefree and uninhibited then.

Jonathan's thoughts next turned to the spring the fever hit. It started first among the slaves and quickly spread to nearly everyone in the whole area. Cholera was no respecter of persons. Doctors had no answers, and slowly and painfully people died. No home was spared. His mother had kept the children confined to the house, but they still had come down with it. Jonathan could remember his brother, Edward, had been the first to come down with it, and then his sister, Sarah. His mother had worked night and day trying everything she could to save them, but nothing seemed to help. Jonathan couldn't remember anything about it because he too was critically ill. He later was told about Edward's and Sarah's deaths. It had taken three months for him to fully recover, and he was like a little lost puppy without Edward and Sarah. Both his mother and father became overly protective of him until he finally went away to college. Neither of his parents ever fully got over having lost their children.

It was during college that he had met Amelia for the first time. His roommate had insisted that he go home with him for a weekend to meet his little sister. He was standing in the library when she came so gracefully floating into the room; her raven-black hair fell like ringlets of satin gracing her blue-green gown. She wore no jewelry except small, dangling silver earrings that glittered and danced near her lovely white cheeks.

Jonathan was so taken aback by her astonishing beauty that he was wobbly kneed and tongue tied. Oh, how her brother had teased him afterwards.

It was love at first sight for Jonathan, and Amelia seemed equally as smitten. She was truly a budding beauty at sixteen, three years younger than Jonathan. Dinner that evening found them both barely able to eat, and they sat there sneaking quick, shy glimpses of each other. That was the beginning of a four-year courtship, which involved many love letters, walks through the gardens, parties, and dances. Over the years Jonathan had spoiled Amelia by giving into her whims and wishes. He worshipped the ground she walked on, and she knew it.

Their wedding had been the memorable event of the year. It was a garden wedding with hundreds of guests from both sides of the family, as well as friends and neighbors from miles around. Amelia's dress was of white satin, with a v-shaped bodice waistline and bell-shaped sleeves. It was adorned with tiny pearl beads down the front and a full bell-shaped skirt, which was popular.

After the wedding, there was a marvelous feast followed by dancing that lasted well into the night. Their wedding had been followed by a wedding trip to Switzerland and many of the major cities of Europe. They were gone six months, and Amelia was well into her pregnancy with Johnny Boy before they returned. What a happy time that had been.

Johnny Boy's birth had been such an exciting time. Even with the anxiety of Amelia's delivery and the joy of his newborn son, Jonathan had been nearly as exhausted as Amelia. He had secretly vowed he would never put her through such an ordeal again, but her first loving words to him had been, "I am ready to give you a daughter." That she had done eighteen months later. They had been so happy, but that had all changed now. The war had done that. It would never again be the same, and now Amelia was leaving.

Jonathan began to think about God. Was there really a God, or was it just a big hoax? There were times when he felt God was very near, and at other times, he seemed to be so far away. He wanted to believe so badly, but his nagging doubts always seemed to cloud the issue. The preacher and Billy Joe made it sound so easy. They seemed to get some hidden strength from reading their Bibles. They also had the most logical answers for every problem and seemed to not have a care in the world except to please God. Well, he wanted to please God too, but what did God want of him? If God would just speak to him or give him some sign. It was all so confusing.

Jonathan sat down under a tree and began to cry out to God, whether he was there or not.

"God! I can't go on! It's hopeless! There is nothing left worth living for, God! I can't even die! I am so miserable, and no one seems to understand. God! Please help me! I need you."

With that Jonathan's heart burst, and he began to sob uncontrollably.

He couldn't remember when he first felt God's presence, but he became distinctly aware that God was there and speaking softly to him.

"Jonathan, I am here. I have always been here just for you. I have been waiting for you to want me and really need me. Do not worry about Amelia. I have work to do in her life also, but she is not ready. Her time is coming. Just be patient, my son."

Jonathan looked around to see if the preacher or Billy Joe was playing a trick on him, and he suddenly had the most wonderful sense of peace. His heart was just bursting, and yet he felt subdued. God had called him "my son." God was there and was in control. He was confident God had really spoken to him, and he was not to worry about the future.

Sometime later Georgiana found her father sitting under the tree so lost in the presence of God that he did not respond when she called to him. She quietly sat down beside her father and put her arms around him, and he began to cry and laugh in uncontrollable joy and didn't fully understand why.

Georgiana stroked her father's head, brushing the hair from his forehead and said, "Momma is just confused, Daddy. She had such high expectations. This has all been a severe shock to her."

For a long time, they just sat and clung to each other in silence. Jonathan was trying to think how he could make Georgiana understand his newfound feelings about God without her rejecting him too.

Ben arrived to find them still sitting quietly.

"Mis Georgiana! Yo'r mother sen' me t' tell youse she be all packed and ready t' go, an' it's time for youse t' come."

"Ben, tell Mother I have decided to stay here with Daddy; he needs me," Georgiana replied.

"Youse kno,' Mis Georgiana, yo' momma, she can't

travel alone. She' be real angry wit' youse. Youse had better come now."

"Ben, our family has been separated for five years now, and it is going to take time to get back together. Tell Mother that if she insists on going to Aunt Birdie's, she can just ask Mammy Lou or someone else to be her traveling companion."

Amelia was shocked and believed that Georgiana's refusal to go with her was again the work of that abolitionist, Billy Joe. Upon Amelia's insistence, Mammy Lou hurriedly packed her few belongings and left her husband, Toby, and their new home to go with Amelia.

The Turning Point

Even though it was now late in the afternoon, if they hurried, they might still catch the evening train to Savannah. Amelia would wire Aunt Birdie to have someone meet them at the train upon their arrival.

Amelia and Mammy Lou left in a cloud of dust as Ben drove the matched bays in a frenzied effort to meet the train. Mammy Lou's voice could be heard above the pounding hooves, berating Amelia for deserting Jonathan in his time of need.

"W'at youse go'in off to Birdie's fo' when youse sup'osed to be w'it you' hus'ban'? W'at kin' a wife is youse t' cut'n run at fi'st sign of t'ouble? Tho't ole Mammy Lou raised youse bet'rn nat. W'at would yo' mommy say? Lawd, I'se glad she ain't here to see dis. Why, sh'd turn o'ber in 'er grave, she would."

"Mammy Lou, you hush your mouth, or I'll sell you down the river. It's none of your business what I do," countered Amelia.

"Youse ain't sellin' ole Mammy Lou now'ere. I's 'Free Issue' now, and I's can do any thin' wh'teve I's wants, an youse can't stop me. And don't youse fo'get it. Ole Mammy Lou is 'Free Issue'! I's can get's right out dis h're bug'y, and I's can go's right back t' my Toby an my own house w'ere I's b'longs. Y's can't stop ole Mammy Lou no mor.'"

"Mammy Lou, you can't leave me now when I need you. You are the only friend I have until Jonathan stops all this foolishness and starts being my husband again, running Castlemont as it is supposed to be run."

"J'st how is Castlemont su'pose t' be run, Mis Amelia, da way's youse wan it or t'way's Mastuh Stevens wan it? Who'da head of dis here fam'ly an'way? Youse got y're high and mi'ty ideas, and youse want ev'body t'do's wat youse want. Ain't Mastuh Stevens s'pose t' be da head of dis here fam'ly? W'at youse try'in to w're da pants f'r? Youse is da wife; youse is su'pose to h'lp y're hus'ben, like ta Lawd said, an here youse is runin' off like some spoilt chil.' Lawd a m'rcy, I tho't I'd ra'sed ya be'trn nat."

"Mammy Lou, you hush your mouth. I don't want to hear another word out of you. I am going to Aunt Birdie's, and that is that! Jonathan is just not the same man I married, and until he comes to his senses, I will just have to stay at Aunt Birdie's."

The rest of the trip to the train station was done in complete silence, both women pouting and looking straight ahead. The train had already pulled into the station when Ben swung the racing team and buggy around the corner to stop before the waiting train. He quickly unloaded their luggage as Amelia purchased tickets. There was no time to wire Aunt Birdie, for the conductor was calling, "All aboard. *All aboard!*"

It was early evening, which meant they would arrive in Savannah during the early morning hours. Since it was after the dinner hour, the dining car was closed, and all they could get was a cup of coffee. In their hurry, neither Amelia nor Mammy Lou had thought to prepare a lunch basket for their trip. They also soon discovered that all the beds in the Pullman sleeping cars were full, so they had no other recourse but to sit up all the way to Savannah. Not being in the best of moods, neither woman had much to say, and each chose to sit sullenly and stare out the window waiting for the other to break the ice.

Mammy Lou could be heard mumbling under her breath about her back hurting and how it was all Amelia's fault. Amelia just stared out the window and pouted.

The sun was just peeking over the horizon when the train pulled into the Savannah station. It had all the makings of a hot sultry day, and both women were exhausted. It took some time before Amelia was able to hail a carriage and driver to take them out to Aunt Birdie's house, which was on the outskirts of the city. To add to Amelia's frustration, the driver twice took wrong turns and had to backtrack. It didn't help to have Mammy Lou constantly reminding her that "Ta Lawd be a punish'n youse for be'in such an un'grat'ful wife who'd run'a'ay from her po'r hus'ben when he needed youse. Serv' youse right if' Birdie would turn youse out."

Aunt Birdie lived in a large plantation-style home with a wide-pillared veranda across the front. She loved the spacious gardens and the several live oak and magnolia trees. A white picket fence enhanced its beauty. There were the customary servant quarters in the back by the stable and carriage house. It had been her parents' townhouse and gathering place for all of the relatives. The upper two floors housed the seven bedrooms, each having a private dressing room.

Birdie's Negro servant, Big Jim, met them at the door and called one of the maids to take their luggage and another to let Aunt Birdie know they had early morning guests. Birdie was always a late riser and didn't like to be disturbed until mid-morning.

Big Jim led them into the parlor and called for tea and rolls. It was the first time that Mammy Lou had been a guest, and side-long looks from Big Jim let her know that she was not to get uppity in this house. She might be Free Issue, but she was still a darkie and had to obey the proprieties. Aunt Birdie was a lady of standing in Savannah, and she did not serve darkies in her parlor.

A short time later, Aunt Birdie came hurriedly down the stairs, not having taken time to fully prepare herself for the day. It was easy to tell that she had hurried into her clothes, and her hair was not fully combed.

"Why, Amelia, what brings you here at this early hour? I must apologize for not having Big Jim meet you at the station, but we didn't know you were coming."

"I am sorry to burst in on you unannounced like this, Aunt Birdie, but there was nothing else I could do. I just couldn't stay at that terrible place another minute." Amelia burst into tears.

Mammy Lou, in disgust, decided it was time to quietly slip out to the kitchen where she knew she would be welcome. Aunt Birdie rushed over to the settee and threw her arms around Amelia.

"My dear, what in the world has happened? Come to Aunt Birdie now, and tell me all about it."

Aunt Birdie was Amelia's mother's sister and had never married, although many a young man had tried to win her affections. As a young woman, she had been engaged to a fine young man of good standing and family, a banker's son. A week before their lavish wedding, she had been jilted, and the young man had run off and married her best friend, who was to have been her maid of honor. Aunt Birdie had never gotten over it and never again desired marriage. Instead she chose to be a mother hen to every forlorn chick and wayfarer that came along. She had been left a large legacy, which provided for her very well. She chose to live a modest, comfortable life and enjoyed her independence. Birdie was not a beautiful woman, but her graciousness made her very attractive.

During the next two hours of tears and cups of tea, Amelia poured out her heartbreak and frustration, of course blaming Jonathan's stubbornness and Billy Joe's abolitionist ideas as the prime cause. Asking her to live in a darkie's house. Turning the plantation over to be run by darkies. Having a school to teach the darkies to read and write. A church where the darkies sat together with the white folk and ate at the same table. Not building the mansion first so as to be ready for her return.

Finally Amelia had cried herself out in complete exhaustion. Aunt Birdie had listened quietly and had occasionally cooed, "Oh, you poor, poor girl!"

Amelia finally asked if she might go up to her room and rest, and suddenly Aunt Birdie was jolted with the reality that all the beds in the house were being used by the wayfarers who had come to her door.

"Oh my! What shall we do? All the beds are full. I just can't ask my guests to leave. Oh my! I guess I could have Big Jim put up some cots in the basement. Maybe one of the guests will be willing to move down there and let you have their room."

Amelia was so exhausted and embarrassed that she, like any wayfarer, had just burst in on Aunt Birdie's gracious hospitality unannounced. She had to confess she did not have any money to stay at a hotel, all of which only enhanced her humiliation. She could just hear Mammy Lou say, "Serves youse right, runn' way f'om yo're hus'ben when he need youse the mos.' Dat man, all he been th'ough after all dis time, and here youse runin' 'way. God be apunishin' youse like he should."

Amelia told Aunt Birdie to not bother her guests even though she resented them being there. She and Mammy Lou would stay in the basement for a few days until a room was available.

Sleeping in the cool basement with Mammy Lou was one of the most humiliating experiences Amelia had ever had. She was used to lavishly furnished bedrooms, with servants to turn down her bed, prepare her bath, and lay out her clothes, and having a private dressing room. Here she was with a makeshift cot, no privacy or bath, and having to listen to Mammy Lou's constant barrage of caustic remarks and overpowering snores. Life was fast crumbling around her, as she was unable to get her rest and was too humiliated to eat properly. She felt life was falling into an endless dark pit with no possible way out.

Jonathan awoke to the shouting and gunfire of the Ku Klux Klan nightriders, which was accompanied by the screams of terror from the former slaves. He burst out of the house to be confronted by the burning of a huge cross in the central compound and another burning up the way before the church. The nightriders, dressed in their customary white hoods and robes, were shouting threats and firing pistols. Suddenly Billy Joe appeared, and they focused their attack on him, beating him to the ground before they rode off into the night. Ben and Toby carried the unconscious Billy Joe into the cabin, and Asa was sent for the doctor.

Georgiana and the preacher arrived, and Georgiana, in tears, fell down beside Billy Joe's bed and began a careful exploratory examination of his injuries. Sarah arrived with a pan of hot water, and someone else brought another light. Billy Joe had been pistol whipped, as well as beaten with a horsewhip. He was covered with blood, and some of his wounds were starting to turn black and blue.

Georgiana carefully washed his face and checked for broken bones. Jonathan and the preacher were doing their best to quiet the hysterical Negro community.

Two hours later, Asa returned with Dr. Watson saying that twice he had to hide out because the roving nightriders had passed by. Dr. Watson gave Billy Joe a complete examination and determined there were no broken bones. He did, though, have to sew up several of the wounds. Billy Joe regained consciousness with a moan and tried to sit up, only to be held down by Georgiana and the doctor.

The next morning the preacher discovered a paper tacked to the door of the church with the following pronouncement:

> This church will burn down
> If any nigger enters its doors
> Or tries to go to school here

Billy Joe, Jonathan, and the preacher immediately called the council together to discuss the situation. The Negro community was in a state of alarm and near hysteria. They remembered too well the threats of harm and death the nightriders had shouted the night before and the attack of Sherman's army.

Billy Joe, with a throbbing head, addressed the council.

"We cannot buckle under to the Ku Klux Klan. Our nation has just fought a great costly war so all men could be free. That includes you folks. We must continue to fight against this kind of terrorism. We must continue our progressive ways at all costs.

"Everyone shall be welcome at church as we had planned, and we shall have school for everyone. Remember the words of our Lord when he said, 'Pray for your enemies' (Matt. 6:44). What that means is that we are to pray for our enemies' 'salvation.' Therefore, I suggest that every evening before bedtime we all gather at the church to pray for them and ask for God's protection. 'If God is for us, who can be against us' (Rom. 8:31)."

The meeting was temporarily interrupted with the

arrival of Sheriff Johnston, who offered Jonathan his condolences, saying he heard about the raid in town from Dr. Watson and came out immediately. He then began his questioning of everyone.

"Did anyone recognize any of the Klan? Maybe a horse, the sound of a voice, a physical description, anything at all?"

Jonathan stated that he remembered that the one who seemed to be the leader was small in stature. "He was the one who kept shouting, 'Kill the niggers! Kill the niggers!'"

Billy Joe concluded the meeting by telling everyone to continue as they were before the nightriders came. There would be armed guards posted around the houses and church at night, but they must not give in to the harassment of the Klan.

The sheriff reinforced Billy Joe's statement by saying, "The army has been called in to put down the Ku Klux Klan throughout Georgia, and any captured Klansmen will be facing a lengthy prison term."

Over the next months, there were further threats by the Klan, but no physical or bodily harm took place, except the burning of several small outbuildings.

Billy Joe, Georgiana, and Jonathan often talked long into each night, with Jonathan occasionally interjecting a word but mostly listening. Billy Joe told them about his childhood, him being an only child growing up in Ohio. He told how distraught and lost he had been when both his parents died. His father had been killed in a farming accident, and his mother just seemed to lose all interest in life and pined away until she too died in a few short months. He told how lonely and lost he felt when he stood at his parents' graves for the last time just before the neighbor drove him to the train station. He had been so frightened, being a twelve-year-old boy traveling all the way from Ohio to Mobile, Alabama, alone on the train with no one to talk to.

His Aunt Martha and Uncle Oscar had met him at the train station. He had never seen them before, and it seemed so unreal to be going to the home of total strangers. All he knew about them was what little his mother had told him.

Learning to live in the South had been a trying experience. He had fought many fights over kids laughing at the way he talked and calling him a Yankee. He told them how he went to the university and then entered law practice in his uncle's law firm. When the rumors of war began to escalate, he and his uncle had many discussions about the "right of secession." It was a hard decision to make. He knew that by going to fight for the Yankees, he would be considered a "copperhead," or snake of the worst kind. He would be fighting many of his personal friends, but he had felt keeping the nation together was more important than "states' rights" and personal friendships. He also knew the South could not stand without the economic support of the North.

He would never forget his uncle's parting words as he left to go north. "Billy Joe, remember you are fighting to save the nation, as well as the South." It was with a heavy heart that he had made that long trip north to enlist with the Yankee forces in Washington. At first he had been suspect and thought of as a possible spy. If it had not been for his uncle's prominence and respect, plus other letters of introduction, he probably never would have been accepted.

Billy Joe did not elaborate about his part in the war except to say that he was never involved in the actual fighting. He picked up the story with the war's end. He was at loose ends because he had gotten word that his uncle and aunt had died and that the law firm had closed. He had aimlessly climbed on his horse and started the long trek south trying to search out in his mind just what God had in store for him. Somehow he wandered into Castlemont and just knew he was supposed to stay and help Jonathan for as long as he felt he was needed.

He went on to talk about his relationship with God and about his views about the reconstruction of the South. He felt the South had to diversify, develop different kinds of industry and crops, and change its attitudes about its traditions and proprieties. There was a need to break down the social caste systems of both the Negroes and the whites. They needed to develop a vision for the future rather than live the laissez-faire status they loved so well.

Over the coming days, Georgiana and Billy Joe continued talking, sometimes over tea or during long walks. They began to realize that they had many things in common such as music, literature, and their progressive ideas. They even talked about how someday they would like to find someone to marry and have a family of their own. Georgiana talked about her widowhood and her sense of loss. They talked about their hopes and dreams of a school and education for the former slaves. They felt a common bond developing between them that at times was mystifying and exciting.

More and more they enjoyed just being together. They began to realize that they were seeking each other out and making up special excuses to be together. They especially enjoyed horseback riding over the plantation and their leisure walks in the moonlight along the quiet river, sometimes hand in hand. It was there beside the river that Billy Joe took her in his arms and kissed her for the first time. When he tried to apologize for his brashness, she quietly touched his lips with her finger and then kissed him back.

"Oh, Georgiana, you are so beautiful. I'm beginning to care for you a lot."

"And I'm beginning to care for you too, and I'm surprised since it hasn't been that long since I lost James. It feels so good to be held again."

"And I like holding you too. I like it a lot." He kissed her again, and then they began to stroll along the river bank arm in arm.

They also talked about their individual concerns regarding Amelia and Jonathan. They wanted them to once again experience the happiness that they were beginning to share.

They also decided that a search for a teacher must begin right away so school could start right after the harvest season. Under the laws of emancipation, all Negroes now had the right to learn to read and write.

Many Southerners were still opposed to the abolitionist idea, fearing Negro retaliation and their wanting equal rights.

Jonathan had been very subdued and given to long periods of staring into space since Amelia had stormed out. Even Benji had trouble drawing him out.

"Mastuh Jon Jon, whar your momma go?" Benji asked one day as they were sitting under the tree at their favorite fishing hole.

"She went away, Benji."

"Don't she like it here no mo'?"

"She is just upset right now. Things just are not like they used to be."

"Wh't do youse mean, Mastuh Jon Jon? I do't see nothin' dif'ren't!"

"Well, you see, I am different. I only have one arm now."

"But, Mastuh Jon Jon, you can't he'p dat! Youse is jist t' same. 'Sides, I likes youse just t' way youse is!"

"Thank you, I wish everyone felt that way."

"Yo'r momma mus' be a funny lady. My momma, she likes me wh'n I gets hurt. She al'ays hugs me an' fusses o'er me. Sometimes it's most em-bara'ssin',' and ta' other kids da laughs a' me a squirm'n wh'n Mamma's a kiss'in.' Is dat t' way youse feel, Mastuh Jon Jon?"

"Sometimes, Benji, sometimes."

"Mastuh Jon Jon, don' your momma wan' t' lib in my gran'pa's house? My poppa, he say yo'r momma, she likes t' lib' in big fan'y houses, wit' darkie servants and' stuf' like dat. She don' feel righ' in o'r little house. Is that righ,' Mastuh Jon Jon?"

"Something like that."

"Mastuh Jon Jon, why is som' folks p'or, an' others ain't? Why is som' white folks so mean to black folks? My poppa, he say som' folks is b'rn mean, but God, he make ever'body, do't he, Mastuh Jon Jon? Did God do som'thin' wrong?" the inquisitive Benji said.

"No, Benji, God didn't do anything wrong. It is man who is wrong. God meant for everyone to be special and to get along and love each other, but man became selfish and greedy. Man wanted to control things and not do things the way God wanted them done. So man began to tell lies, cheat, steal, and think of himself as better than others, even better than God and the angels.

"That is how we came to have slaves. White men stole the black men from their homes far, far away in a land called Africa, brought them to this country, and made them slaves. Your grandpa and grandma came from Africa, where they were taken from their homes and families by slave traders. They were sold to wealthy white men in this country and made to be slaves to work the plantations. Their freedom was taken away from them, and that is why we had this terrible war where so many people were killed fighting for what they believed was their states' rights," said Jonathan.

"Mastuh Jon Jon, is I yo'r slave?"

"You used to be, as were all the Negro folks that lived here at Castlemont," Jonathan said.

"Did you kno' t'was wrong t' make us slaves, Mastuh Jon Jon?"

"Yes, I knew slavery was wrong, but everyone had slaves. My grandfather and father had slaves here, and I inherited the plantation with the slaves. I didn't know what else to do. There just seemed to always have been slaves," replied Jonathan.

"If youse kno'd it was w'ong, then why youse do it, Mastuh Jon Jon?' said the ever-probing Benji.

"Because I thought I would not be able to farm the plantation without slaves."

"But Mastuh Jon Jon, w'ats youse goin' t' do now dat all da slaves b'en freed? My poppa, he say we's just goin' t' work f'r youse as always."

"The only difference now, is that everyone will get paid for their work, and the money they earn can be spent any way they chose to spend it. They can also go to school and learn to read and write, like you will be doing in a few weeks. That is, as soon as we find a teacher," said Jonathan.

"Is youse goin' t' school t,' Mastuh Jon Jon?"

"No, I have already been to school, and I already know how to read and write," replied the amused Jonathan.

"My poppa and momma, da say da is goin' to school at night 'cause da wants t' read and write," Benji proudly boasted.

The shadows began to fall, and it was time to go home.

Jonathan, Billy Joe, and Georgiana continued to discuss the need of a schoolteacher for the upcoming school session, which they wanted to begin shortly after the end of harvest. They decided that Billy Joe should escort Georgiana and Clara, the fifteen-year-old daughter of Tom and Dolly, who could act as a chaperone for Georgiana while traveling with Billy Joe to Savannah. Georgiana would visit with her mother while Billy Joe made inquiries about a schoolteacher. The Negroes who were not involved in the harvest were assigned to the work of building a house for the schoolteacher.

Jonathan and Toby saw them off to the train. It was a beautiful autumn morning with a soft breeze blowing and not a cloud in the sky. They could see the field hands working at bringing in the harvest on several plantations along the way, yet many of the once fertile fields were still a mass of weeds and young pine trees that had sprung up. They had last minute messages for Amelia and Mammy Lou, and everyone laughed when the engineer blew the whistle and Clara screamed. This was her first train ride, and it was very exciting, yet frightening, for her.

It was a long trip to Savannah, and it was not unusual for the train to be late. Billy Joe sent a wire to Aunt Birdie letting her know they would arrive on the late evening train. The train ride was uneventful, and they spent much of their time just enjoying each other's company, talking about just what kind of teacher they needed and the future of Castlemont. Since this was Clara's first train ride, she stayed glued to the window, overwhelmed by the passing countryside.

Billy Joe was insistent that the top priorities for the teacher were to be that he or she should be a Christian, well educated, and open to teaching Negroes. Other attributes must be patience, understanding, and a real love for teaching. Under no circumstance was the teacher to be abusive.

Georgiana was amazed at this man, Billy Joe. He was so sure of himself, with a fine mind for detail, yet so compassionate for everyone, especially the former slaves. She knew she was falling in love. This time it was different than when she had fallen in love with her late husband, James. Her love for Billy Joe had a greater sense of maturity about it.

Billy Joe and Georgiana were bombarded with questions from Clara as the train passed through the various towns, cities, and countryside. She had no comprehension that there were so many people in the whole world, and she would hide her eyes in fear as the train crossed any big river. This was a big adventure for a fifteen-year-old Negro girl.

Georgiana talked about Aunt Birdie in an attempt to prepare Billy Joe for their first meeting. Aunt Birdie had devoted her life to caring for the less fortunate who constantly beat a path to her door. It was not unusual to see her carriage passing through the dark streets in the black of night on some mission of mercy, nor was it unusual to find anywhere from one to five strangers living in her spacious home. No one was a stranger to Aunt Birdie.

The thing Amelia hated most about staying with Aunt Birdie was Aunt Birdie's insistence that she participate in her weekly ladies' Bible study and prayer time. That was another thing that bothered her. They were always talking about reading their Bibles and quoting some scripture, and she couldn't even remember where she had left her Bible. She hadn't read anything in it since her childhood confirmation classes. Reading Sir Walter Scott, Shakespeare, Charles Dickens, or another of the great classics was far more important in her social standing than reading the Bible. Religion was religion, and there was nothing personal or real about it. It was a social tradition. Everyone went to church, that is, everyone who was anyone. Aunt Birdie and her cronies were going too far. They were fanatics. That could lead to a person becoming unbalanced. They were just religious do-gooders who liked to flaunt their wealth.

Yet there was something unusually special about these ladies. Amelia began to think back over the few meetings she had attended in the past. She couldn't remember any of them saying a bad word about anyone. They expressed what appeared to be a genuine, sincere empathy and concern for a certain lady of questionable background who was seriously ill. They took turns, it seemed, sitting up with her, and praying for her or reading the Bible to her.

She tried to remember where she had put her confirmation Bible. Georgiana had also used it for her confirmation classes. It must have been destroyed when Castlemont was burned.

Amelia and Mammy Lou had been at Aunt Birdie's for about six months when one day Aunt Birdie came rushing into the parlor with the news that Georgiana was coming for a visit. At first Amelia was ecstatic, but then she began to have foreboding misgivings. Immediately a number of questions raced through her mind. Why was she coming? Had she finally come to her senses also and left Castlemont, or was she coming to try and talk her mother into coming back to Castlemont? She had no intentions of ever going back to Castlemont until Jonathan came crawling on his knees and begged her to return having rebuilt the mansion just as it had been.

That evening Big Jim announced the arrival of Georgiana. Amelia was so excited that she rushed to meet her until she saw her adversary, Billy Joe.

"Georgiana! What is he doing here? What is the meaning of this? You traveling alone with…with this man? Have you lost your mind? Where are your priorities?"

Amelia had completely overlooked the presence of Clara in her contempt for Billy Joe.

"Mother! What are you talking about? I have Clara with me, and Mr. Barker accompanied us so he could search for a teacher for our school while you and I visit."

"Our school! What do you mean, 'our school'? Have you joined forces with this abolitionist? Georgiana! There is not going to be any school at Castlemont. Is that clear?"

There was a long, silent pause, finally broken by Aunt Birdie hustling through the door, having just arrived home from one of her many outings.

"Georgiana! How good to see you! Have you come to

visit your mother? She needs you, my dear. She has been so upset and lonely."

"It's good to see you again, too, Aunt Birdie," said Georgiana. "I can't stay long. I did come to visit Mother, but Mr. Barker and I have to also find a teacher for the Castlemont school."

Aunt Birdie exclaimed, "Oh my! We do have a bit of a problem. We will have to find a place for you to stay. You see, my dear, right now all my beds are filled with guests. I'll tell you what. I will send Big Jim over to Margaret Tolliver's. You remember her, don't you, dear? She is such a dear friend of mine, and I know she has lots of room."

Billy Joe spoke up. "Aunt Birdie, forgive me for being so forward, but no one has told me your last name so that I could address you properly. You will not have to find a place for me. I plan to take a room at the hotel."

"I'm sorry, Billy Joe. May I formally introduce you to my very special great-aunt, Miss Bernadine Montague of Savannah. Aunt Birdie, I want you to meet Mr. Billy Joe Barker of Castlemont."

"Oh my! I haven't been called Bernadine since my formal coming-out party when I was sixteen. Mr. Barker, all my friends just call me 'Aunt Birdie.' The name was given to me by my little brother when he was learning to talk. He couldn't say Bernadine, so he called me Birdie. The name stuck, and I have been Birdie ever since."

Billy Joe soon made his departure to the hotel, and Aunt Birdie ordered tea for everyone. Clara found her way to the kitchen and the comfort of Mammy Lou and the kitchen staff. There was a somewhat strained tension as tea was served because Amelia was defensive about the real reasons for Georgiana's visit.

"Mother, have you been enjoying your stay here with Aunt Birdie?"

Aunt Birdie chimed in before Amelia could answer. "Oh, we have been having a marvelous time, but I must say your mother has been somewhat upset by seeing all the occupational soldiers about town. Oh yes, and your mother seems to enjoy our ladies' Bible study and prayer time so much. You must come with us, too, my dear."

Amelia was speechless and nearly fell out of her chair. There had not been one minute of joy for her since she had arrived in Savannah.

Amelia wanted desperately to ask all kinds of questions about Jonathan and the workings of Castlemont but did not want to show her real concerns. Georgiana changed the subject and began to talk about the past times of fun she had had when she visited her Aunt Birdie.

Big Jim soon returned from Mrs. Tolliver's with the news that Georgiana and Clara were more than welcome and that Ole Sam was bringing the carriage to pick them up. Georgiana was relieved that she could escape the feelings of tension she felt in her mother's presence and would be able to get some rest.

Billy Joe checked into the hotel and immediately began to inquire at the desk about the possibilities of any available schoolteachers in the area. The next morning he started the rounds of all the churches in the area to see if any of the preachers knew or could recommend a schoolteacher. After two days he had exhausted all the leads he had and decided it was time to check in with Georgiana.

Georgiana had made it a point to visit with her mother each day, but there always seemed to be so much tension between them now that had never been there before. This bothered Georgiana. She wanted to talk about the family plans for Castlemont as she now understood them, but she did not feel at liberty to do so. Aunt Birdie had insisted that she also attend the ladies' Bible study.

Georgiana was fascinated by the openness of Aunt Birdie and her friends. They made God seem so real and personal that Georgiana found herself wanting to have that same kind of relationship for herself, in spite of her mother's aloofness. She was intrigued at the way they just seemed to talk to God when they prayed. It seemed so personal, as if God was right there in the room with them.

During the evenings at Mrs. Tolliver's, Georgiana felt at liberty to talk freely about "the relationship," and Mrs. Tolliver was refreshing, gracious, and open to Georgiana's questions.

"I have discovered that God is very real and personal. I have learned to believe his Word and accept it implicitly in faith. I take it just as it is, even though I don't always understand it or see immediate evidence. I know he is real and faithful, and his word is true. He answers our prayers when we learn 'his will.' We learn that by reading his Word. I know that God wants to do a wonderful thing for Jonathan and Amelia, but he is waiting for her to give up her stubborn Southern pride. We have to be willing to humble ourselves and pray, yielding our will to his will, before God will intervene in our lives."

Georgiana was sitting in quiet reverie and speculation when Old Sam ushered Billy Joe into the sitting room. Georgiana jumped up and gave Billy Joe a big hug as she cried out, "Oh, Billy Joe, I am so glad that you have come. Mrs. Tolliver has been telling me about her relationship with God and how he answers her prayers."

Billy Joe handed his hat and coat to Old Sam and greeted the ladies.

"Billy Joe, Aunt Birdie and Mrs. Tolliver talk about having a relationship with God the way you and Preacher Rogers do. Do you think it is possible for me to discover such a relationship for myself?"

Billy Joe seated himself next to her and, taking her hand, turned his full attention upon her. "Georgiana, I know that you know that there is a God. Are you willing to surrender your life to him, and are you willing to devote your life to living just to bring glory to him and not yourself?"

Georgiana sat quietly for a few moments. "I want to, but I don't know how."

"It is very simple. In fact, it is so simple that most people think it is ridiculous. All you have to do is invite God to enter your heart in a meaningful, simple prayer of surrendering your will to him. Something like this: 'Father God, I invite you into my heart to become my personal Lord and Savior. I confess that I have sinned against you and lived my own selfish will and not yours; therefore, I have failed you, and that is sin. From this day forth, I commit my life to living just for you, that your kingdom will come and your will be done in my life, that my life may glorify you and bring to me peace and joy regardless of the circumstances, and that the Holy Ghost may have the liberty to flow through my life to reach other people for your glory and their salvation.'"

Georgiana had quietly prayed the prayer after Billy Joe and after a few moments raised her tear-filled eyes with her heart overflowing. Mrs. Tolliver could hardly contain herself and sent Old Sam to have Aunt Birdie come over so that they all might praise God together. The evening was such a joyous occasion.

The talk later had turned to the search for a schoolteacher. They had all bowed their heads and asked God to hear their prayer and send the right teacher to them. Praying was a new experience for Georgiana, and she didn't know if she could do it right but decided that if she meant business, God would understand. An hour had quickly passed by when Georgiana let out a startled cry.

"I can't believe it! I don't understand! I believe God is asking me to be the teacher. That is ridiculous! I have never been a teacher."

Billy Joe, Aunt Birdie, and Mrs. Tolliver said a simultaneous "Praise the Lord." Billy Joe then confided that he had believed for some time that God wanted Georgiana to be the teacher all along. "I don't know anything about being a teacher."

Mrs. Tolliver said, "Georgiana, God only asks you to be willing, and he will do the rest. Besides, your students don't know anything about being students, so you can all learn together."

Georgiana was in a state of shock, and Billy Joe sat there laughing.

"Isn't God wonderful, Georgiana? He doesn't waste time when we let him have his way, and besides, you can now apply all that you have learned at the university. Well! It is late, and I had better go back to the hotel because tomorrow we will have to go to the stores to get the school supplies and teacher manuals."

Again they bowed their heads to thank God for Georgiana's newfound relationship with God and his calling her to be the teacher.

The next evening they had dinner at Aunt Birdie's in preparation for their returning to Castlemont the following morning. Everyone was exuberant except for Amelia, who was withdrawn and barely touched her food.

"Georgiana, what makes you think you can teach darkies? You know they can't learn like white folks can. You don't even have a teacher's license. You will be the disgrace of the whole county. What will our neighbors think? It is just not right."

Everyone had stopped eating with this outburst, and there was a heaviness in the air for the rest of the dinner.

"Mother, regardless of what you or anyone else may think, I know I have been called by God to teach, and no one is going to stop me. I must listen to God and no one else."

Amelia jumped to her feet. "Georgiana, have you totally lost your mind? What have these people been telling you? 'God told you to do this, and God told you to do that.' That's so much poppy-cock! No daughter of mine is going to be a schoolteacher to a bunch of darkies."

Amelia threw down her napkin and stomped out of the room. Everyone was momentarily stunned, and Georgiana began to quietly sob as Billy Joe and Aunt Birdie gathered around her.

A little while later, Billy Joe and Georgiana decided to go for an evening walk so they could talk in private. The growing sunset found them strolling along, hand in hand, when Billy Joe stopped and drew Georgiana to him, encircling her in his arms.

"I am becoming very fond of you. May I have your permission to ask your father if I may court you?"

He then gently kissed her, and she whispered her consent and found herself responding to his kisses as she snuggled against his broad chest.

The next morning Mammy Lou announced that she was going home with Billy Joe and Georgiana. She had done her part in helping Amelia get to Savannah, and now she wanted to go back to her Toby and her very own new little house at Castlemont. Billy Joe and Georgiana made a few last-minute purchases before they all boarded the train to return to Castlemont. Amelia had remained in her room brooding and had not come down to even say good-bye.

The return trip home was relatively uneventful. Billy Joe and Georgiana mostly talked about her newfound faith and the prospects of the new school. They decided that Billy Joe and the preacher would at first help with the teaching and give lessons on the Bible. They had no idea as to how many children to expect in the beginning.

They would have some evening classes so the adults could attend school after work. In the meantime Clara and Mammy Lou talked about the sights they were seeing along the way.

From time to time Billy Joe and Georgiana's hands seemed to find each other as they gazed into each other's eyes with thoughts of their growing relationship and the future. Both began to understand that they had fallen in love.

Jonathan and Toby met them at the train depot that evening, and Jonathan was eager to hear news about Amelia. He had secretly hoped that she had returned with them. The wind seemed to go out of his sails when told about her attitude. But all agreed that in time, and with God's help, Amelia would come to herself and to God. Toby and Mammy Lou were excited to see each other again.

Billy Joe and Georgiana had been home about a week when he and Jonathan were riding their horses out to survey the progress of the work on Castlemont.

"Mr. Stevens, it has been nearly a year since I first met Georgiana, and I have grown very fond of her and would be honored if I could have your permission to seriously court her."

"Well, I would be honored to have you marry my daughter, but I have just one request, and that is that you drop the 'Mr. Stevens' and call me either Dad or just plain Jonathan. If we are going to be family, we should be on a first name basis. Of course, that is if Georgiana agrees to being courted. By the way, are you sure Georgiana meets all your original high expectations for a wife?"

"I am absolutely sure of it Mr....I mean Jonathan. I couldn't be happier."

"Well, then, maybe we ought to start thinking about building another house. Have you given any thought as to where you might want to build?"

"I will have to talk it over with Georgiana one of these days, and we will decide together."

Amelia tossed and turned in fretful sleep. She was dreaming of hundreds of Negroes coming from every direction to the school, and she was trying to drive them away, listening to their mournful cries. She then saw a giant of a figure, radiating in brilliant light with outstretched arms, hovering over Georgiana as she was waving to the children to come to the school. Another of Amelia's dreams was about being all alone in a misty fog enshrouding a field. She could hear people all about her, but when she called out to them, no one responded.

Amelia woke with Aunt Birdie tugging at her arm. "Amelia, dear, Amelia, honey, wake up. You have been having a terrible dream, shouting and crying so loud you woke up the whole household. Wake up, now!"

Amelia sat up in a state of alarm.

"Oh! Mammy Lou, I mean, Aunt Birdie, I had the most dreadful dreams. Hold me close, Aunt Birdie. I am so afraid."

The two women fell into each other's arms as Amelia began to sob hysterically.

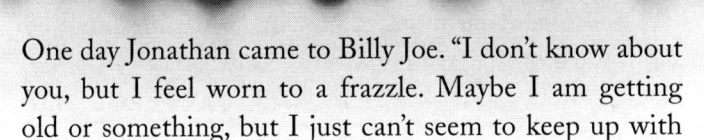

One day Jonathan came to Billy Joe. "I don't know about you, but I feel worn to a frazzle. Maybe I am getting old or something, but I just can't seem to keep up with everything that needs to be done."

"I know just what you mean. I feel that same way. What we need is a good business manager who can keep track of each farm's earnings, wages, and share of the overall taxes and make sure the harvest was properly sold and accounted for and the monies distributed properly."

"Do you know of anyone who might fill the bill?"

"Well, in college I had this friend who was an accountant and who was also working on his law degree. Bart would be perfect if we could find him and talk him into coming here. After all, Castlemont is a cooperative, and he wanted to be an executive in a large corporation."

"Where do you think he might be?"

"Well, before the war started, he had established himself in the Sloan-Benson Office of Accountants in Mobile, Alabama."

"Well, it's worth a try to find him, and if he is not available, then maybe he can recommend someone else. We have got to have some help. Why don't you take some time off and go see if you can find him or someone who can help us out?"

Since Jonathan was the plantation owner, it was only natural that he be the general overseer of the total operation. He would be the one to help the twelve appointed tenant farmers choose their crops and tell them when to plant and harvest. The crops would be rotated so as not to wear out the soil.

Each tenant farm was a plot of about one hundred acres. Each of the farmers would receive one third of the harvest for himself. Jonathan would receive one third also as the landowner, and the other third would go to pay the wages of the carpenters, blacksmiths, bricklayers, field hands, and the ladies who did the household chores of each farm. If a farmer wanted or needed extra help, he would pay their wages out of his share. To their knowledge, there had never been a plantation or farm set up to run like this except the Davis Bend Freedman's Colony.

Billy Joe was to use his law background to see that everyone was treated fairly and that all the legal matters were taken care of properly. It was not long before other plantation owners were seeking out his counsel as well.

After a tiring trip to Mobile by train, Billy Joe arrived to find that the Sloan-Benson Office of Accountants was no longer there, and no one in the area knew anything about Barton Sloan. Billy Joe started walking the streets and asking everyone for any knowledge of Barton Sloan.

The war had been over for many months now, yet the streets were still filled with people begging for food or any form of work that they might do. The hard part for Billy Joe was seeing so many people maimed in one form or another. They had little chance of ever becoming anything but street beggars if they had no family to help them.

"Billy Joe! Billy Joe Barker, is that you?"

Billy Joe stopped, looking all around trying to search out the familiar voice. Then he noticed a man sitting on the ground with no legs below his knees, haggard, unshaven, emaciated, and dressed in rags.

"Billy Joe, it's me, Barton Sloan. Don't you remember your old classmate?"

Billy Joe was speechless, and his eyes filled with tears. Could this really be Bart, the fun-loving yet serious classmate? Bart, who had such a bright future as a corporate executive, sitting there disfigured and destitute? Finally Billy Joe found his voice.

"Bart, what in the world happened to you? How did you end up here on the street?"

"Well, Billy Joe, no one seems to want a legless corporate executive or even a legless anything. Everyone seems to act like I was the one who started the war in the first place and caused all this carnage that you see all around here."

"Bart, I have been looking all over for you this past week because I have a job just for you."

Tears began to trickle down the stunned face of the hopeless Barton Sloan.

"Billy Joe, don't be kidding me." I know no one wants the likes of me."

"I do have a job for you, Bart. I'm serious. I know your fine mind and capabilities. You are just the man we need at Castlemont, and legs do not matter."

Immediately others began to gather around to beg Billy Joe for jobs and help. After talking some more, Billy Joe picked his friend up and carried him down the street to a restaurant so Bart could eat a good meal and they could continue their talk undisturbed. Billy Joe told Bart all about Castlemont, what they were attempting to do there, and how badly they needed him. Bart was amazed and gradually began to relax and become excited about the upcoming prospects.

"Billy Joe, this must be God's answer to my prayer. I have been so without any hope, and here you come looking just for me. I can hardly believe it."

"Bart, Castlemont is a new experiment in doing things God's way. It is a little like the Davis Bend Freedman's Colony. We have set up the plantation on the structure of the parable of the talents and the twelve apostles. Mr. Stevens, the owner, will still be the owner and overseer. Twelve of his former loyal slaves were chosen 'apostles' to be the tenant farmers, each having about one hundred acres to farm. They will be able to hire people to help them. Each tenant farmer will receive one third of the harvest, Mr. Stevens will get one third, and the other third will pay the wages of the hired people."

"That sounds like an exciting adventure you have worked out, but how do you hold it all together?"

"Each of the twelve tenant farmers also forms the general council, which meets briefly once a week with Mr. Stevens and me so that we all will be marching to the same drum beat for the whole plantation. You can see why we need a business manager like you."

"I will say it will be a challenge. How does Mr. Stevens feel about this, being a large plantation owner and used to doing things his own way?"

"Well, Bart, at first Mr. Stevens was very much against it, but being a war casualty like yourself, he knew he had to make changes. It helped a lot when he finally accepted the Lord as his Savior and began to trust in God's word."

"Is everyone on the plantation a Christian, Billy Joe?"

"Not everyone yet, but we are working on it."

"How do the neighbors feel about what you are doing?"

"Some are taking a wait-and-see attitude; others are outright hostile about it. We have had several visits from the KKK. Most people think that given time the whole idea will fail in one way other the other."

One week later everyone at Castlemont turned out to greet the return of Billy Joe and the new business manager. There was a lot of cheering until a hush fell over the crowd as they became aware of Bart's handicap. Jonathan was overwhelmed to see someone in a seemingly worse physical handicap than even he.

After the formal introductions were all made, plans began to take shape as to how they all could make Bart comfortable. He would need a special office and a conveyance of some kind to help him get around. The carpenters and blacksmiths soon had their heads together as plans began to unfold to the making of a chair with wheels and a special pony cart. For the immediate future, Jethro was appointed to be Bart's man, or valet, and help him get situated with a place to stay. Jethro would also be in training as an assistant to Bart as the plantation manager.

Over the next several days, Jonathan, Billy Joe, and the council met with Bart to bring him up to date on the restructure and new format of the workings of the new Castlemont. The ever-present Jethro was there at Bart's side to be of assistance in any way necessary. Bart was amazed and soon became very excited that he had been chosen to be a part of such a progressive operation.

Their plan for Castlemont was certainly way ahead of the times and would take close watch to make sure that it would work and that nothing would be allowed to fall through the cracks. This had to be a good example to all the surrounding neighbors. They soon realized that there was a need for Castlemont to have a corporate office with offices for Jonathan, Billy Joe, and Bart, as well as a place for Bart to live. The site was selected, and the carpenters set to work.

It was not long before Jonathan and Bart became close friends. Their handicaps made for a bonding of like minds, and they enjoyed spending time swapping war stories. Since they both liked to fish and had Benji and Jethro to help, the four were quite often found fishing down at the river under the shade of one of the giant oak trees.

One day a stranger came driving up the lane with a tired horse and old buggy and introduced himself as Doc Morgan. "Doctor Watson in Cedar Creek told me that you folks might be in need of a part-time resident doctor out here. I am a doctor, and as you can see I am somewhat limited in what I can do. He too had lost a leg in the war and was looking for a place where he could carry on his practice in a limited way. He was also recovering from his addiction to strong drink. He was willing to be their doctor for little more than room and board.

Doc did not hesitate to let it be known that he had lost his family and medical practice due to his addiction and would not allow spirits of any kind in his presence.

Since he had heard that Castlemont was some kind of a Christian community, he had hoped that he might fit right in since he too had become a Christian.

Castlemont's population had grown to well over one hundred residents, so there was a need for a doctor to be nearby. After a meeting with the council, Doc Morgan became Castlemont's resident physician. Word quickly spread, and people from other nearby plantations began to come to see Doc. Within two weeks, the resident carpenters erected a small office building near the church and new corporate building for the good doctor. Castlemont was growing and growing.

Doc, Jonathan, and Bart quickly became friends because of their shared disabilities and began to kid each other as to who was the most handicapped. They would often be found together in the evenings drinking coffee and playing cribbage or dominoes. Billy Joe was glad to see their friendship developing because that left him free to devote more of his attention to Georgiana. Mose and Maudie were soon assigned as Doc's assistants. Mose was to help Doc get around to see patients, help Doc in and out of his buggy, and care for the horse. Maudie, who was well known as a mid-wife and for her healing herbs, would be his nurse. Benji soon let the good doctor know that he was going to become a doctor when he grew up and was often found going with Doc as he made his rounds.

During one of the council meetings, Bart brought up the need for Castlemont to have its own general store. The Ku Klux Klan was still active in the area and threatened the former slaves when they went to town for their supplies, even stopping them on their way home and destroying what they had purchased with their hard-earned money. The stores were also prone to charging the Negroes higher prices. A community store would be located by the church and school and would be a service to the whole area. Therefore, the search was started to find a store manager, and plans began to take shape to build the building.

One evening as the men were enjoying their nightly game of cribbage, there was a knock at the door and someone calling for Dr. Morgan. A family from a nearby plantation was sick and needed the doctor immediately. Doc called for Mose and Maudie to join him, and seven-year-old Benji insisted that he had to go as Doc's assistant. This amused Doc, but he took him along anyway. You could never start too young training someone to be a doctor.

After careful examination of the patients, Doc determined that their symptoms appeared to be that of typhoid fever and immediately declared their home to be quarantined. He then sent Mose and Benji back to Castlemont with the news of the outbreak. Since little was yet known about the fever, most of the people were thrown into a near panic. Soon three other families in the area came down with the fever, and everyone knew that they were in for a full-blown epidemic.

Jonathan took charge and decided that the schoolhouse should be made into a temporary hospital, and Georgiana's house next door would be made into a central kitchen and dispensary. All the cases of the fever would be moved to the schoolhouse so Doc could treat everyone more easily. Billy Joe, Georgiana, and the preacher became the unofficial nurses in the temporary hospital. Most everyone knew that the fever could be fatal or at best take up to four weeks to make a recovery.

Enough had been learned about typhoid fever to know that cleanliness was mandatory in helping to ward off the disease. Therefore, the council was assembled and instructed to inform everyone within their jurisdiction to thoroughly clean their houses and to wash their hands often, as well as boil their drinking water.

It soon became apparent that the schoolhouse could not hold all those who were sick, and the church was prepared to also become part of the hospital. By the end of the second week, three people had died, and six others were gravely ill. Billy Joe sent word out to other areas letting them know of the outbreak and requested more help in fighting the epidemic. Aunt Birdie sent two doctors all the way from Savannah to help, and other volunteers arrived to give the exhausted staff a much-needed rest. Doc was near exhaustion and often awoke to find that he had fallen asleep as Mose and Maudie took him to more and more cases in the area that had developed. The epidemic finally ran its course with seventeen people having died and others taking months to recover.

It had been two and a half years since Jonathan had returned to Castlemont, and they had just brought in their first big harvest with everyone's help. The sawmill was thriving, and they had built most of the houses that were needed throughout the plantation. Only Jonathan's house remained to be built.

Even though the area had gone through the typhoid epidemic and Castlemont had been the central point in curbing the epidemic, there had been numerous threats against Castlemont. The threats were targeted against Georgiana, Billy Joe, Preacher Rogers, and Jonathan in particular. Several gunshots had been fired at the new schoolhouse, and once someone had attempted to burn down the building.

Emotions were running high, so Billy Joe had contacted the sheriff, who in turn contacted the occupational army of Georgia. A platoon of Yankee soldiers had arrived and set up camp beside the schoolhouse to ensure peace. Daily the soldiers were ridiculed by passersby and at night were the victims of random gunshots, which wounded one soldier. The governor then ordered an additional three platoons of Yankee soldiers into the area, whose job it was to patrol the whole area night and day looking for and arresting troublemakers. Their main objective was to protect the homes of the Negroes from the intimidations of the Ku Klux Klan. The Negroes of all ages were eager to have the opportunity to go to school, and they were going to get their chance.

The soldiers soon captured six members of the Klan and put them in jail to await trial for harassment, attempted murder, and destruction of property. The members arrested were a banker, a barber, a grocery store owner, and three neighboring plantation owners. The big problem would be to find a jury in the area that would not be biased so that they would get a fair trial.

The Negro population was in a confused state as to what to do. Their freedom was still so new, and many did not know how to or were afraid to stand up for their rights. Threats had been made to all of them that if they or their children attended the school, they could expect that all kinds of things would happen to them, such as their houses or crops being mysteriously burned or the women folk being raped. Any man caught traveling on the roads would be beaten or killed. It did not help that so many of the Negroes were so superstitious that their minds ran wild.

Billy Joe called a meeting of the council, and he and Preacher Rogers again reinforced to the people the importance of not giving into the intimidations and said that they should still send their children to school. Each family was promised to have guards watching their homes, property, and roads around the clock. The occupation army even had undercover agents infiltrating the meetings of the troublemakers, so they would be captured before they could do any trouble.

Georgiana and Billy Joe decided to use the method of "each one teach one" to start with since everyone was a beginner. Each child who came to school would be encouraged to go home and teach the rest of the family what they had learned that day. That way the older members of the family would be prepared to learn when they attended the evening classes for adults after the fall crops had been planted.

The first day of school started with forty-three excited but somewhat shy and intimidated students. Three had been threatened and one beaten on their way to school as a warning to all the rest as to what they could expect in days to come. The soldiers stood guard around the schoolhouse.

There was also a special surprise when Governor Bradley made an unexpected visit as a way of throwing his support toward this new venture in education. He let it be known he personally opposed the education of Negroes, but because of the new laws, he had to support it. He was also curious to see if Negroes could really learn to read and write. He knew Castlemont's school was to be the first Negro school to open in the state.

All of the students were amazed that they would each have an assigned seat and a slate of their very own. Since there were more students than desks, some of the students were asked to share. Some of the students even tried eating the new sticks of chalk. They didn't know what to think when Georgiana told them that they each would have their very own reading book with their name written in it.

Georgiana began the day by reading from the Bible and giving a short prayer. Then each student was asked to stand and tell everyone his or her name. The overly excited Sammy blurted out, "I kn'os all of dem a'redy, Ms. Georgiana," and the kids all laughed, which seemed to relax them some.

Georgiana had to go over some new and basic rules about staying seated in their desks and not talking out loud without first raising their hand and asking for permission to do so. Little Elijah several times got up and began to wander around the room curiously looking at pictures on the wall. He would touch this and that, oblivious of Ms. Georgiana and the rest of the students.

Recess was a new experience for the students, and most of them didn't know what to do with themselves or what was expected of them. Billy Joe was on hand and began to get them organized in several games that they all knew. The soldiers were on special alert because of the threats that harm would come to the students.

Story time immediately became a favorite time of the school day as the students all gathered around Georgiana's chair, sitting on the floor or on nearby desks. After Georgiana had read to them, they talked about the story. Many of the children had failed to bring a lunch, so Georgiana and Billy Joe, anticipating this might happen, handed out sandwiches and apples.

Later, after lunchtime, Georgiana again had each student stand and tell the class what they would like to become later in life. Benji was the most excited and enthusiastically stated that he was going to grow up to become a doctor just like Doc. Most of the class had no idea what they would like to be except maybe to help their parents at Castlemont.

The next day the students returned to school excited about being able to tell their siblings and parents about what happened in school the day before. Every morning a little time was given for the students to share. This was a real eye opener to Georgiana and Billy Joe as to what transpired in the homes during the evening. During the first few days of school, several mothers lingered to observe the school procedure. One could tell they were also eager to come to school.

Both Georgiana and Billy Joe, along with Preacher Rogers, were encouraged by how quickly the children were learning. Most of them soon learned their alphabet and were beginning to sight read the simple words in their readers. Everyone had mastered being able to count to ten. Several of the students expressed talent in art, and everyone was encouraged to draw pictures of their school to take home to their parents. Since everyone, regardless of age, was a beginner, a lot of their learning was done by rote.

The Thanksgiving season was quickly upon them, so time was spent reading stories and talking to the children about the first Thanksgiving and their own need to be thankful. Of course they were all thankful for their school, and some expressed thanks for their church. Others talked about their families having a special Thanksgiving dinner, but none of them had ever remembered having turkey and wondered why eating turkey was so special and what it tasted like. They talked about having chicken for their Thanksgiving dinner because there were no turkeys available, but they would have the usual vegetables that make for a special dinner. Several families were going to share a meal and eat together.

Outside threats against the school had slacked off drastically as the community adjusted to the school being there. Of course, the military presence was a big help also. After Thanksgiving was over, Georgiana began preparing the students for the Christmas program. Everyone was to have a part in the program. There were songs to be learned and poems to recite, as well as a simple play about the nativity. None of them had ever seen a Christmas program, let alone been a part of one. Patiently Georgiana read the story of the nativity from the Bible, and they talked about it.

Each passing day some time was spent in making decorations for a Christmas tree and the schoolroom and even for them to take home with them. None of the students had ever had a Christmas tree with presents, so this was going to be a new experience for them.

Parents and older siblings were growing anxious for the great day to arrive. Georgiana and Billy Joe had sent money out of the corporate fund to Aunt Birdie for candy, oranges, and small gifts for all the students and siblings yet at home. The older students made strings of popcorn to decorate the tree, and several had a hard time not eating the decorations. Billy Joe had some of the men help in putting together a manger scene for the Christmas play.

The Christmas program became the talk of the whole community. None of the Negroes had ever seen or participated in a program, but some of them had received simple gifts from their plantation owners. The parents were so proud that their children were going to be in the program, and even some of the adults were asked to participate.

Amelia's Struggle

It was the late fall of the year that Amelia and Mammy Lou had arrived unannounced on Aunt Birdie's doorstep. Amelia was so angry and confused because no one seemed to understand or seemingly even care about her personal wants or feelings. She occasionally received a letter from Jonathan and Georgiana but never with the news she wanted to hear.

She loved Jonathan, but she just couldn't go back to Castlemont until he had built her a new house equal to the mansion she was used to before the war. After all, she was a lady of social stature in the community. She had her pride, and she was not about to give up her lifestyle regardless of what other people thought. Jonathan just had to come to his senses.

It was most humiliating to have to be beholden to Aunt Birdie for everything since Jonathan had not sent her any money of any real significance. She seldom ever left the house except to go with Aunt Birdie to her Bible study and occasionally to church on Sunday. Oh, how she hated those Bible studies. Those ladies just did not understand, always talking about "letting the Lord have his way, talking to and hearing from God." Oh! If she didn't get out of there, she was going to go crazy.

Yet she did recognize that they seemed different: happy, at peace with the world, and living with what they called "divine expectancy." They even claimed to have their prayers answered and found exciting new ways to serve the Lord. She certainly didn't have any of her prayers answered. It was so maddening. It made her feel like some kind of a freak because she was not like them.

The thing that bothered Amelia the most was that Aunt Birdie and her little group of cronies were always doing something to help the poor. Why, they even invited them into their homes or would go and sit up through the night with someone who was sick or dying. But they all seemed to be so happy, always singing, praying, or praising the Lord, and of course, reading their ever-present Bibles.

She had to get out of there before she lost her mind, but where could she go? She didn't have any money or other family to stay with. Then there was her memory of Mammy Lou always raving about her not supporting Jonathan and his crazy venture with Castlemont.

One day when Amelia was at her wit's end, Aunt Birdie had her sit down, and she began to tell Amelia about her own personal life story. Aunt Birdie had been raised in a wealthy family, the only girl who had every whim and want granted by her overindulgent parents. Birdie was not physically a beautiful woman like Amelia, but her beauty was found in her kind, loving spirit, a beauty from within that drew people to her.

"I had become engaged to marry Tom, a longtime friend. We had grown up together as neighbors, and everyone just assumed that we would marry someday. We had so much in common, and all our friends were glad when our wedding date was finally set. Mother and I, along with several of my best friends, worked hard to make it a very special wedding day for Tom and me.

"The invitations had gone out, and the wedding party had been selected. It was a very exciting time for me, and I was so much in love with Tom. Then, just three days before the wedding, Tom ran off and married Sally, who was to have been my maid of honor in the wedding. I was crushed, and for weeks I hid myself in my parents' home. In my dark depression, I would not see anyone. My only prayer was, 'Why, God?'

"Finally one day I opened my long-neglected Bible and began to read, 'Come to me, all you who are weary and burdened, and I will give you rest. Take my yoke upon you and learn from me, for I am gentle and humble in heart, and you will find rest for your soul' (Mt. 11.28–29). It just seemed to jump out at me as if it was meant just for me.

"That was the turning point in my life as I began to pray just as Jesus had prayed, 'Not my will, but your will be done' (Mt. 6:39). I then began to read my Bible daily and began to take note of things that I believed to be God's will. Finally the day came when I surrendered my heart to the Lord, as well as my right to marriage, and I had a great sense of peace for the first time.

"Gradually God led me to new friends and new opportunities to express my life, which took the place of what I had thought marriage would be. Each new day was a new opportunity to surrender my will to the Lord and discover a new opportunity to serve him. I am so glad that I am free to serve the Lord and that financially he has blessed me so I can be a blessing to others. I would never want to go back to what my life had been when I was going to marry Tom. I would have missed out on so much."

Amelia sat quietly for a long time, and then she began to ask questions.

"Don't you care about your social status, what people think about you, or what they are saying about you?"

"No, I don't, because they are not in control of my life. I only care about how I can please my Lord. Social status has no lasting value because it is always changing by the selfish whims of those involved in it. There is nothing sacred or secure about it to give you peace."

"But don't you miss the parties, the theater, balls, and concerts? The important people that make up our social status?"

"Those things are nice, and I participate as I want. But my real joy is in helping those in need. You remember Jesus saying, 'Whatever you did for one of the least of these brothers of mine, you did it for me' (Mt. 25.40). And he spoke of us caring for the sick, feeding the poor, clothing those who have nothing, and visiting those who are in prison, even the giving of a drink of water in his name. There are so many people out there in our community who have reached their rope's end and do not know where else to go. Have you ever thought about what it must be like to be so sick you couldn't move, and there is no one there to even wash your face and give you a drink of water? What it would be like to have no one to talk to who might give you some hope? You and I have always had family we could count on, but there are many people who have no one. Those are the ones that Jesus wants us to care about."

"But didn't Jesus also say, 'The poor you will always have with you'?"

"That is right. That only means we will always have opportunities to be a blessing to someone on our Lord's behalf."

Late in the night, as Amelia was sleeping, she again wrestled with who was really in control of her life and happiness. She was not used to praying, but in desperation she began hesitantly to cry out to God. The still, small voice of God's spirit began to speak to her through a long forgotten scripture she had learned in catechism class as a young girl. "Be still, and know that I am God" (Ps. 46:10).

"'Be still, and know that I am God.' How do I do that?"

"Think on these things, whatever is true, whatever is noble, whatever is right, whatever is pure, whatever is lovely, whatever is admirable—if anything is excellent or praiseworthy. Think about such things" (Phil. 4:8).

"What about what I want, the things that have always been important to me?"

"Be still, and know that I am God. I have come that they may have life, and have it to the full" (Jn. 10:10).

"How do I know that you are God?"

There was suddenly a bright light followed by a voice. "This is my beloved Son, hear ye him."

Amelia suddenly fell on her face, shivering even though it was a warm night. In her troubled dream she saw herself opening her Bible and beginning to read, "The acts of the sinful nature are obvious: sexual immorality, impurity and debauchery; idolatry and witchcraft; hatred, discord, jealousy, fits of rage, selfish ambition, dissensions, factions and envy; drunkenness, orgies, and the like. I warn you, as I did before, that those who live like this will not inherit the Kingdom of God. But the fruit of the Spirit is love, joy, peace, patience, kindness, goodness, faithfulness, gentleness, and self-control. Against such things there is no law. Those who belong to Christ Jesus have crucified the sinful nature with its passions and desires" (Gal. 5:19–26).

Amelia continued in her struggling battle of wills, her will against God's will, her social status and traditions against God's love and sacrifice. Finally Aunt Birdie gently shook her awake, for she had been crying out in great sobs.

"Oh, Aunt Birdie, I have been having this terrible dream about God demanding me to give up everything I treasure or I will continue to be lost. Why would a loving God be so selfish that he has to have only his way?"

"Because he loves you so much that he wants you to have everything that he has to offer that will give you the greatest joy and fulfillment in life. God's ways are not man's ways, Amelia. His word says, 'God so loved the world that He gave his only begotten son, that whosoever believeth in him shall not perish but have everlasting life' (Jn. 3:16). God's ways are always best for us."

"How can I have this new life?"

"Amelia, salvation is God's gift of grace. The scripture says, 'Believe in the Lord Jesus, and you will be saved' (Acts 16:31). That is just the beginning. After being saved initially, one must live the surrendered life. By that I mean that every day one is to seek God's will for our lives through prayer and the study of the Bible. Those are some of the ways God speaks to us. Being saved is not enough. That is only the beginning. Learning to live in God's will is where the joy and richness of life is found. Let's say you committed a crime worthy of death, but the king or a judge comes and pardons you. He saves you. But clearly you owe him your life. Now you could choose to not become his servant by choosing to live just the way you alone want to and have been, but a king or judge really has rule and authority over your life. In your gratitude, I would think you would want to worship him."

"I want that new life for myself."

Together Amelia and Aunt Birdie knelt down beside Amelia's bed, and Amelia surrendered her life to Jesus. She began to pray, "Lord, you know I don't know how to pray like Aunt Birdie, but I want you to know I am willing to learn. First, I want to be like Jesus, who prayed, 'not my will but your will,' for my life. You know that I have always wanted to be in control and have everything my way. This means, Lord, I am surrendering my need for a fancy big mansion and the latest fashion in clothes because I have put my values in what I have thought others expected of me. Help me to learn to see people as you see them, and let my relationship with you be more important than any social status. Please help me become the wife Jonathan now needs, and may I be willing to allow him to lead our marriage if he will have me back. Lord, I want to learn to serve you and know that I am doing your will in my life. Amen."

Several weeks had passed since Amelia had surrendered her heart to the Lord. She was at peace and a different person, as she and Aunt Birdie spent much time in prayer and Bible study together at the beginning of each day. For the first time in her life, Amelia was interested in learning to cook and sew. She and Aunt Birdie had some good laughs at some of her first culinary failures. Now she was so sorry she had ever doubted Jonathan.

A letter arrived from Georgiana bringing them up to date on all the happenings at Castlemont, especially the upcoming Christmas program at the school. "Aunt Birdie, I just have to go back to Castlemont and be there for that Christmas program. Would you be willing to go with me since Mammy Lou isn't here to be my traveling companion? Wouldn't it really be exciting if we could surprise them?"

For a second Aunt Birdie was flabbergasted, but then she also began to get excited about the prospect of the surprise.

They set about making their arrangements, packing their trunks, and purchasing their tickets for the journey. Amelia was truly a new person, so excited, looking forward to seeing Jonathan again and learning all about the new Castlemont and what God had in store for them, and especially for her.

The day finally arrived for the school Christmas program. It was a beautiful winter day with the sun glistening through the leafless trees. The morning began with a beautiful frost covering everything like a fine blanket of cake frosting. The horses frisked around the corrals, kicking up their heels, and the crows called to one another from the trees.

The children were so excited it was nearly impossible to conduct classes, so Georgiana, Billy Joe, and the preacher took turns telling stories and reading to the children. There were some last-minute line rehearsals and some final touches on the decorations. The children did a lot of speculating about what was in all the prettily wrapped gifts under the tree. They took a long lunch hour and extra-long recesses. The students were then sent home early to get ready for the big program that evening.

The program began promptly at seven that evening with an overflowing crowd, for everyone in the whole community had come. This was truly something new for all of them, and they could barely squeeze everyone in. Preacher Rogers began the program with a prayer, followed with the Christmas carol "Oh Come All Ye Faithful." Amelia and Aunt Birdie slipped in the back unnoticed.

Several of the students got stage fright so badly they could not remember their lines and burst into tears. Georgiana took time to give them each a hug, and the program moved on. More Christmas carols were sung, and finally it was time for the nativity. Jed and Sarah played Joseph and Mary, with baby Jenny being the baby

Jesus. Bubba, Jacob, and Elisha were the shepherds. Benji and young Toby were dressed up as sheep, and the three wisemen were made up of three of the older boys. When everyone was in place, Neb and Clara stood up and sang "Sweet Little Jesus Boy." The program ended with everyone joining in singing "Silent Night," followed with a few tears and sniffles among the crowd.

Billy Joe and the preacher then began passing out the gifts and candy, making sure that everyone got something. Suddenly Billy Joe stopped and stared at the back door, seeing Amelia and Aunt Birdie. Georgiana followed his gaze and screamed, "Mother!" The whole crowd began to praise the Lord afresh. Jonathan worked his way through the crowd back to Amelia as she rushed into his arm. He could see right away that his wife appeared to be a different person from the last time he had seen her.

Before the evening was over, Amelia let it be known that she was home to stay. She just wanted to find her place in the development of the new Castlemont. Mammy Lou could be heard over the noise of the crowd shouting, "Praise da Lawd! Praise da Lawd, home at las.' My girl is hom' at las.'"

The party went on for another hour until it was getting late, and families began gathering up their children and heading for home. Someone had put on a fresh pot of coffee for those who were going to remain with Jonathan and Amelia. There was a lot of catching up to do, and no one seemed to want the evening to end.

Amelia shared the story of her conversion and let them all know that she was home to stay. She and Jonathan sat holding hands and from time to time gave each other a reassuring hug. She also shared that when she first went to Aunt Birdie's, she hated going to her Bible studies and thought they were some kind of religious fanatics, but gradually she found that the other women had a special contentment and joy in life that she desired. After she found Jesus for herself, she looked forward to the Bible studies and the fellowship of being with other Christians.

Finally the hour grew late, and Jonathan asked the preacher to lead them in a closing prayer before they took themselves off to bed. The holiday season was truly a joyous occasion for everyone at Castlemont. Every evening the people gathered in groups to sing carols and share their thoughts of Christmas. One of their main topics of conversation was regarding their first-ever Christmas program at the school.

It wasn't long before everyone began to notice that Aunt Birdie and Preacher Zedikiah Rogers seemed to be found talking together a lot. Knowing grins were passed around. Amelia had lots of questions regarding the school and the new Castlemont and just how she could fit in the whole picture. She seemed to take a particular interest in the possibilities of the new store. Georgiana and Aunt Birdie temporarily moved in with Mammy Lou and Toby so Jonathan and Amelia could have some time alone together in Georgiana's house. Jonathan and Amelia talked at length as to the further development of Castlemont, and he was interested in her ideas, especially from a woman's point of view. They explored the possibilities of the store further because there was a definite need for one, and Amelia seemed fascinated by it.

Several weeks had passed, and each evening Billy Joe and Georgiana, Jonathan and Amelia, and Aunt Birdie and the preacher, along with Doc Morgan and Bart Sloan, would gather together to discuss the future of Castlemont. Most of the meetings were also attended by some of the council as well. Everyone was amazed that Aunt Birdie was taking such a personal interest in Castlemont.

As they pooled their thoughts together, a vision of a local town called Castlemont began to surface. They already had a school, a church, a doctor's office, an attorney, and an accountant, along with a general mercantile store in the planning. Doc raised the issue that he needed to expand his facilities to include a small hospital with several beds and a surgery and to have a trained staff to run it. There was even speculation that they needed to put out a search for a trained nurse to help Doc in the surgery and hospital.

Amelia was so excited about the store that she nearly forgot about having a fancy house of her own. The group spent time at each meeting praying because they wanted to be in God's will and not rush ahead of his blessing.

It was finally decided that before the spring work began, Jonathan and Amelia needed to return to Savannah, stay at Aunt Birdie's house, and explore the area stores for ideas on what they wanted for their own store. Aunt Birdie would go with them because she was so well acquainted with the city and personally knew most of the general store owners as well as the wholesale warehouses. They needed to know just what to stock in their store and learn where the best warehouses were for making their purchases, as well as to establish a line of credit with the bank. Aunt Birdie agreed to become a co-signer. Particular interest was to be given to store arrangement that was appealing and serviceable, as well as the size of the building they would need.

They arrived back in Savannah on a Sunday evening, and for the next week, they spent their days going from business to business. Amelia carried a note pad to write the details of all they were learning. Jonathan surprised her by taking her shopping, and together they picked out a new wedding ring to replace the one she had had to sell to get enough money to return to Castlemont.

It was like a second honeymoon for them.

"You know, Jonathan, I am beginning to feel like a teenager again, like when we were courting. I was so madly in love with you, and I was so afraid that you felt I was too young and immature for you."

"Sweetheart, you do not know how many nights I laid awake thinking about you. You had nothing to fear."

"I don't know how I could have been so lucky to have snared you," said Amelia.

"What do you mean, you snared me? I worked hard to fight off all the other guys that were lined up drooling over you."

Amelia blushed and gave Jonathan a hug.

They took time to go to the theater, as well as to eat at several of the nicer restaurants. Amelia was at first interested in the latest fashions being worn by the upper class ladies. Then she had to remind herself that fashion did not make the person. She began to realize that Castlemont offered the more important things of life's realities. They also attended church services with Aunt Birdie and realized how much they missed their own services back home.

One night after they had prepared for bed, they lay awake talking.

"You know, Jonathan, being a Christian is exciting, yet somewhat sad. All my life I thought only of myself. Now I am learning that as a Christian I find my joy in putting others first, and that means all the people at Castlemont."

"What exactly do you mean?"

"Well, let's talk about our house. I always loved the mansion; I was so proud of it and gave no thought to the humble slave quarters. They were slaves, after all. Now they are people with the same wants and the same desires that we have. You know, Jonathan, I don't think Jesus would want to live in a big mansion while we lived in little unpainted shacks. Therefore, when we build our house, I want it to be nice, but it certainly does not need to be a mansion. I already have a mansion prepared for me in heaven."

"That is sure the truth, but what do you have in mind?"

"Well, I have been thinking of maybe just a modest two-story home with three or four bedrooms upstairs and a nice dining area, with a parlor and living room. We don't need a grand ballroom or fancy winding staircases. I don't plan to have a whole house full of servants as we used to have. I just want a nice home where people can find peace, joy, and comfort. Maybe we could even call it our haven of rest."

"When we get the store up and running, we will make plans to build a nice, comfortable home where we would be proud to have Jesus as a guest."

Amelia became anxious to get back to Castlemont and put into practice all they had been learning about the general store business. She knew Bart would be a lot of help in putting all the details into practice.

They arrived back at Castlemont tired but excited. To everyone's surprise, Aunt Birdie had moved back with them to Castlemont for the time being. The next morning they gathered the group together and shared with them all they had learned and their expectations. First, they had decided that the store building itself would need to be much larger than they had first planned in order to hold all the merchandise they planned to have in stock. They had been able to buy a number of secondhand counters and shelving that were to arrive by train over the next several weeks. They also decided to build living quarters in the back of the store where Amelia and Jonathan could live while the store was being established. Then they could build their own home and let the store manager live in the back of the store. They had also hired an experienced store manager to help get the store started, who would temporarily live with Billy Joe.

As the building began to take shape, neighbors from the surrounding plantations began to drop by and ask questions about the store. They wanted to know if the store would stock everything they needed so they would not have to go all the way to Cedar Crossing to have their needs met. They also wanted to know what the store hours would be and whether they would have to pay cash or would be able to put their purchases on the tab against their harvest check. These were all questions that would have to be worked out.

Four months quickly passed as the store building took shape. Supply wagons began to arrive daily as Amelia and Robert, the store manager, directed the hired help in stocking the shelves. Finally the date for the grand opening was set, which created a special excitement for the whole community.

The doors opened to a big crowd who had come to "their store." The children gathered around the glass-enclosed counter containing many different jars of candy, and each child was given a complimentary red and white barber pole peppermint stick. The ladies oohed and aahed over the many bolts of fabric, ribbons, and lace, as the men gathered around the central stove to drink coffee and talk man talk. Amelia, Jonathan, and the staff were kept busy answering questions and waiting on customers. The day passed quickly, and the staff was exhausted. It was exhilarating to have a dream fulfilled, and now it was time for a celebration of praise.

Six months later, the construction of Jonathan and Amelia's house began to take shape on the site of the old mansion. It would take nearly five months to complete, but it would be a modest home in comparison to most plantation mansions. Since the store was operating smoothly, Amelia could take time each day to be with Jonathan and oversee the construction of their new home.

They had hired an architect from Mobile to draw up the plans, who insisted that their ideas were not in keeping with most plantation homes. Grudgingly he finally consented to give into their concept of what they wanted in a home. After all, they were going to live in it, not the community, and since they were no longer social climbers, their desires were what counted. They wanted a home where if they had grandchildren, they could pop in and out or come stay for a short time. Amelia wanted a home where she could do as Aunt Birdie did and take in people who were destitute for a fresh start in life.

The Wedding

The three years since Jonathan's return to Castlemont had passed quickly. He and Amelia were happily settled into their new home, and the store and school were running smoothly, as well as the rest of the plantation. Billy Joe and Georgiana decided that they wanted to get married, and now was the time to set the date and make the final plans for their wedding. They picked out a site to have their house built on and approved a set of plans so the builders could begin immediately and have it done in time for the wedding. They also made a special trip to Savannah to pick out their wedding rings and for Georgiana to select a wedding dress. It was to be the social event of the year, and not a stone was to be left unturned. Of course, everyone wanted to come, so the question arose as to where to have their wedding.

"If we have it at the church, not everyone will be able to fit into the building, and some would be hurt and feel left out," said Georgiana.

"That would be the same problem if we had it at your

folk's new house. Even their yard is not ready to handle the traffic of a big wedding."

"What do you think about having it down at our favorite spot by the river where we first kissed in the moonlight? That way it will be special to us, and everyone could come. We could have the men bring the benches from the church for the ladies and the older people, and everyone else could either stand or sit on the ground."

"The men could build a lovely arch with a cross, and the women and children could gather lots of wild flowers to decorate it. That way everyone could have a part in our wedding."

"I like that idea," said Georgiana. "What should we do about formal invitations? I know that everyone for miles around will want an invitation, as well as the people of the church. That could be very time consuming and expensive."

"Wouldn't it be fun to do as Aunt Birdie suggested and have someone dressed up as a medieval times town crier and go throughout the countryside announcing our wedding? We could dress up several of the boys and have them go on horseback to all our neighbors with a scroll and make the announcement. I can just see it now, right in the middle of the church service, before Preacher Rogers begins his sermon, have the crier stroll down the aisle, unroll his scroll, and shout out, 'Hear ye! Hear ye! On the twentieth day of June, eighteen hundred seventy-one, in the year of our Lord, at two o'clock in the afternoon, Miss Georgiana Stewart shall be married to Mr. Billy Joe Barker. The wedding will take place in a riverside setting at the plantation Castlemont. Everyone is invited.'"

"I love it. I have never heard of it being done that way before, but then we want our wedding to be different. It would be special," said Georgiana, "Let's do it. I can just see several of the older boys as our town criers. They would love it. Isn't it getting exciting?"

"Now what do you want to do about a reception, because everyone will want to come to that as well?"

"Now that does pose another problem. What do you think about having a good old Southern barbecue? I am sure Daddy would be glad to provide a couple of hogs, and then we could have all the ladies bring a favorite dish. That way everyone could enjoy themselves without putting out a lot of money that we really don't have. Another thing, I want our wedding to be a happy time for everyone to feel included, with singing, games, dancing, storytelling, and maybe even a very brief worship service to especially praise God for bringing us together."

"I like it," said Billy Joe.

"Now we should discuss the wedding party itself. I think I would like to ask Aunt Birdie to be my maid of honor."

"Do you think she might be hurt remembering her own disastrous wedding day?"

"No, I think this might have a special meaning for her, knowing that she is a special aunt and especially since Preacher Rogers will be performing the wedding. You have to remember that there is a special interest budding there."

"Yes, she has made a number of trips back here to Castlemont over the past year just to see how 'everything was developing.' And the preacher also has made several trips to Savannah 'on church business.'"

"Who do you think they are trying to kid?"

"What do you think about me having Bart as my best man, even though he would struggle to walk up there on the rather uneven ground?" said Billy Joe.

"He is your friend and a special part of our community. Several of the men could bring him up just before the wedding begins, and he could stand with his crutches for the wedding. Then he could follow the wedding party out with help in his special chair."

"I wish that Bart could find a wife. He would make a good husband and father. He has such a tender heart, especially for the less fortunate."

"There is still time. Did he ever have anyone special while you two were still in college?"

"Yes, her name was Betty Jo Price. They were getting real close, but then the war broke out. She was from Macon, Georgia. I don't know what ever happened to her."

"Just for fun, let's try to find out and maybe invite her to our wedding."

"Do you think that it would be appropriate? She is probably married and has a family."

"Well, there is only one way to find out. Maybe the preacher knows a pastor in Macon who could do some detective work for us. Let's ask him."

Several weeks went by, and one day Preacher Rogers caught up with Billy Joe and Georgiana with the exciting news that Betty Jo Price was living in Macon and had never married. She was devoting herself to caring for her aged parents. That was all that was needed for Billy Joe and Georgiana to send Betty Jo a special invitation to their wedding with a train ticket. They would sit back and wait to see what happened.

The twentieth of June finally arrived. It was a beautiful day for a wedding without a cloud in the sky. There was an aura of great excitement throughout the whole community. Everyone came dressed in their Sunday best. Some of the men even wore ties, and many of the ladies had made themselves new sunbonnets to match their dresses. By one o'clock people began to arrive.

Georgiana had lots of help, with a gathering of women besides her mother and Aunt Birdie wanting to help her get dressed. Of course, Mammy Lou was there supervising the whole affair; after all, Georgiana was like a daughter to her. Billy Joe had purchased a new suit for the occasion and was being kidded by the men about being nervous.

Promptly at two o'clock, the musicians began the prelude music to settle the people down. A lone violin began the popular new wedding march by Mendelssohn, and the whole audience stood to see the bride preceded down the aisle by three little flower girls and Aunt Birdie. Betty Jo Price had quietly slipped in the back of the crowd unnoticed.

Georgiana made a beautiful bride walking beside Jonathan, clutching his arm and carrying a small nosegay of flowers attached to a small wedding Bible that Amelia had given to her for the occasion.

The ceremony was short, with both Billy Joe and

Georgiana repeating their wedding vows clearly as a number of women dabbed at tear-filled eyes.

The wedding reception took place under the nearby giant oak trees, with everyone laughing and joking about their own weddings and kidding the newlyweds. The afternoon began to cool down, and the musicians tuned up for the wedding dance.

After the first dance led by the bride and groom, Preacher Rogers called for everyone's attention to announce that Aunt Birdie had just consented to become his bride. Everyone began to clap, and a number of "Praise the Lawd's" could be heard. Aunt Birdie blushed and planted a tender kiss on the cheek of the preacher. Bart and Betty Joe were greatly surprised when they first discovered each other and could hardly wait to get a moment to talk. There was a lot of catching up to do, so they quietly drew off to the side of the crowd and became lost in their own little world as the rest of the wedding party went on without them even noticing. They were both amazed that neither had married, and their long dormant love began to be rekindled.

Later that night, Jonathan and Amelia lay in bed and shared their thoughts of the day. "It was a beautiful wedding, and I am so happy for them. But I think our wedding was more beautiful and of course a lot more elaborate. Maybe ours was more beautiful because I have the most beautiful bride."

"You are just being prejudiced, but I love it. Yes, ours was much more elaborate, but that does not make a marriage successful."

"I love you and am looking forward to many more happy years of loving you."

"You know, Jonathan, God has really blessed us. It reminds me of a scripture I read the other day in Psalms 126.3. 'The Lord has done great things for us and we are filled with joy.'"